BATTLE LINES

BOOK ONE IN THE QUEST FOR TRANQUILITY
TRILOGY

Andrew Furstenberg

Table of Contents

Race for Survival

Storm clouds brewed on the dark horizon, but the cheerful inhabitants of the small village called Quinsael hardly cared. They were having a celebration in the town square; food and spirits had been consumed, and now dancing, singing, and flutes and fiddles filled the night air. All were cheerful and content, unaware that their peaceful existence was about to end.

Thanju and Elaine, one of the many married couples in the village, stood near the dancing circle.

Noticing that Elaine was tapping her hands and feet to the music's rhythm, Thanju smiled and asked, "Would you like to dance?"

Elaine stopped and smiled back; even after all their time together, that smile still captivated him. "I don't think so, Thanju."

Thanju offered her his arm. "We haven't danced since before Banju was born. I insist."

With that, they happily joined in on Quinsael's traditional dance. Those around them cheered them on as the climax of the fast song came and they took center stage and danced even more vigorously. Tapping, swinging and twirling became fluid. The end of the song drew near, and everyone around them stopped to watch their elaborate and enthusiastic dance. Now the only dancers, Thanju and Elaine bowed as their companions clapped and hollered.

When the noise died down, one of Quinsael's sentries sprinted to the center of the stage, out of breath, terror in his eyes. "They're here!" he managed to spurt out before collapsing, a spike protruding from his left shoulder blade.

The square erupted into chaos; many screamed, others fainted and still others leapt into action, racing home to grab weapons for the desperate defense of Quinsael.

"They finally found us!" Elaine exclaimed in terror as she and Thanju rushed home. "What're we going to do?"

"We run so we can fight," Thanju said as he dodged a man on horseback heading the other way. They reached their home and immediately ran to the boys' room where their babysitter Wren was rocking year-old Rik, their youngest.

"You folks are back ear—" Wren said, stopping when she noticed the fear on their faces. "What's wrong?"

Elaine took Rik from her, and Thanju led Wren into the kitchen, away from his sleeping sons. "Listen carefully, Wren. They have come, and they will give no quarter. Return home to your family."

Wren's lower lip quivered. "Surely there is something we can do…?"

Thanju patted her shoulder and opened the door. "Run, hide, pray. They are not here for you, but they will kill you if you stay here. Farewell, Wren; I wish you the best."

Wren was on the brink of tears. "You, too, sir."

Thanju sprinted back into the house, grabbing his sword and other supplies left and right. Elaine appeared, Rik still in her arms. "Here," Thanju handed her a potion. "Give this to the boys; it will keep them asleep."

She took it without question and gave a portion of it to Rik. Their eldest son Banju walked into the kitchen, groggy, rubbing his eyes. "Mommy? Daddy?"

Careful to contain his emotions, Thanju knelt down to his two year old son. "Everything is all right, Banju." He held up the vial. "I want you to drink this. It will all be over soon."

Banju looked at him with trusting eyes as he drank the sleeping potion. Within seconds, he collapsed into his father's arms. Thanju placed him in a harness that he then put around his shoulders to keep Banju close to his chest. "Ready, Elaine?"

She nodded, and they hastily headed for the stable. Once on horseback, they sped toward Quinsael's south gate.

"Thanju, you weren't going to leave without saying farewell, were you?" Burdick, his best friend, asked when they reached it. Sword in one hand and spear in the other, Burdick was prepared to defend the south gate until death overtook him.

"Burdick, come with us! There is still time!"

Burdick shook his head. "Nay, my friend; I must stay here and hold them off so you and your family have a chance to escape."

3

Thanju held out his hand, and Burdick clasped it. "Never have I had a friend greater than you."

Burdick forced a smile. "Nor I." Something broke through the barricade behind him—it resembled a coyote, but twice as vicious and made entirely of dark, rough stones. As it lunged toward him, Burdick smoothly spun around, stabbed it with his spear and beheaded it with his sword. Wiping the dead creature's unnatural blood from his face, he exclaimed, "Now get out of here before the rest of them arrives!"

With that, Thanju and Elaine left Quinsael, never to return. Screams and the crashing destruction of the town's gate could be heard as they forced their horses to gallop faster through the dense forest.

The storm was finally upon them. Lightning flashed, thunder roared; the torrent of rain falling upon the trees sounded like a thousand cascading waterfalls.

There was a roar behind them, a sound that made the horses neigh and pick up speed. Thanju and Elaine tried to keep their horses on the trail, but instead the horses ran to the only place they thought to be safe: a large, raging river. The horses came to an abrupt halt in front of it; it was nearly impossible to hear anything except the surging water.

"Thanju," Elaine gingerly handed Rik and his harness to Thanju. "Take the boys somewhere safe and raise them. I'll turn around and distract our pursuers." Her voice was unusually calm, as if she knew and accepted her fate.

Thanju shook his head. "Don't do this, Elaine; they need you."

"They need you more than me. Besides, if I go with you, they will catch us." Another bellow erupted a hundred yards behind them. "Please go before they find us again!" She kissed him. "Goodbye, my husband." She looked lovingly at the boys. "Goodbye, Banju and Rik; perhaps I'll see you again someday." With that, she spurred her horse to turn around and face their pursuers. She saw nothing within the next few hundred yards; she slowed her horse to a trot and drew her elegant, silver sword.

All was quiet, save the pattering of rain on leaves and the persistent growling of thunder.

Suddenly, a black force ran into her horse's chest, sending her roughly to the ground. Within moments she was back on her feet and prepared for an attack. The horse lay writhing, its chest punctured.

"I know you're out there!" Elaine shouted into the surrounding darkness. "Reveal yourself so we can end this quickly!"

A dark cloaked figure materialized ten yards in front of her. "You elves and humans are terribly foolish. We should have known you would do something as fruitless as this," it spat, its voice low and menacing.

"It is such 'fruitless' endeavors that will always set us apart from you," Elaine stated, composed despite her predicament. It could be counted on one hand how many people had survived one-on-one encounters with these creatures.

"And that is why we have so easily killed many of your kin. I realize what you are doing, foolish elf, but your attempts at stalling me with conversation end now."

Elaine braced herself and pointed her sword forward. "Let us finish this, then."

Her pursuer chuckled, spiked bones drawing out of each knuckle. "So be i—" Its comment was cut short as it dodged out of the way of a thrown dagger. A growl replaced its chuckle and it lunged at Elaine.

She slid to the side and hit it in the back with her hilt. The creature instantly recovered and slashed at her chest. Elaine blocked and aimed for its legs, only managing to slash off a bit of cloak before being parried. It was a stalemate; neither one of them could strike a debilitating blow. However, Elaine was aware that she was growing fatigued and had to act quickly. She managed to briefly kick her opponent away, drew a short sword and began fighting with twofold aggression. Her adversary blocked her every attack and was able to cut through her defense, slashing her arms, legs and face. Elaine knew her end was near.

In a last ditch effort, she gathered all of her strength and released it in a merciless offensive that forced her foe to step back and receive multiple stab wounds. The short sword became buried in the creature's left shoulder, infuriating it. Her antagonist roared at Elaine and smashed her right hand with a backhanded strike. Her sword gone and her main sword hand broken and bleeding, Elaine prepared for the inevitable. Nevertheless, she was not going to give in so easily. She jumped onto her opponent, wrenching the short sword out of its shoulder with her good hand and stabbing profusely into its back. The creature screamed and threw her off. Elaine made contact with a tree and crumpled to the ground. It was over.

Her assailant stumbled to her injured form and stamped on her short sword, smashing it in half. The creature knelt down and put its face close to Elaine's so it could hear the satiating sound of her labored breathing. "Have anything to say before I kill you?"

Her voice struggled to come out of her damaged lungs. "Peace will return...and you will finally be expunged from this land!" She plunged what was left of her sword into her killer's side.

It shrieked and thrust its clawed hands into her chest. She was already dead. The creature wrenched its hands out and relished in the falling rain. "And so begins the fall of the slayer's kin." It laughed victoriously and began to rip Elaine's dead body apart from the inside out.

Meanwhile, Thanju's horse sped into the relentless river, and a dark cloaked figure rushed in after them.

In terror, the horse ran faster, but its legs abruptly froze on the other side of the large river. As the horse stopped, their pursuer stopped as well, right in the middle of the waterway.

Thanju drew his bow and aimed at their hunter, who gestured with a hand for Thanju to take his best shot. His arrow radiated a brilliant red. When lightning struck again, Thanju saw a barrier blocking another river from this one. He employed his heightened senses to aim his bow at a weak spot in the barrier and fired.

At first, nothing happened, but then the rumbling sound of snapping wood could be heard over the storm: The second river was pushing thousands of gallons of water through the ever-growing crack in the natural dam.

Seeing what was happening, their pursuer roared and began to sprint toward Thanju, but to no avail; millions of gallons of water hit it like a stone wall.

Thanju did not wait to see if the water was effective; he dug his heels into his horse's sides and continued his trek through the storm.

The Blacksmith

16 Years Later

Since that fateful storm sixteen years before, Thanju had found refuge in a large town called Smith Village. How it acquired that name, no one was sure, but many believed that it was because more than half of its inhabitants were blacksmiths. Some even said that they were the best in the kingdom and were comparable to the dwarves who had roamed the lands hundreds of years prior.

The village was five miles in diameter and was surrounded by a three-meter tall stone wall. Beyond its walls was a forest that went on as far as the eye could see. A river circled around the forest, cutting Smith Village and its neighbor Bootskin off from the rest of the kingdom. Because of this, the Smithian province was often wrongly referred to as an island. Being the furthest northwest and the closest to the Rift that separated Shallor from the Riftlands, Smith Village rarely received visitors. The inhabitants were fine with that; they firmly believed that the less they were involved with "city-dwellers," the better. Crime was minimal, often only occurring when visitors came.

However, there was once every year on a certain day in autumn that outsiders were welcomed with open arms. Hundreds of men, women and children would gather at a giant oak tree located at the center of the village for a festival called the Ponderer's Festival: a contest where storytellers from all over the kingdom would compete to see who could tell the best story.

For some, it was just another excuse to break open kegs of beer reserved for special occasions. Gurst, dubbed the "town drunk," was there every year sitting in his small wooden chair and using his two personal kegs as armrests. His huge round gut could attest to his many years of excessive eating and drinking. "Where's be that Gurath? I want to be enjoyin' my drinks, so I do!"

On the other side of the field, Banju sat on a boulder with his best friend, Terin, and his brother Rik. Banju was a tall, toned, broad-shouldered young man with hazel eyes and short dark brown hair, while his brother Rik had black hair and blue eyes and was shorter and slenderer. This did not bother Rik in the least, however, for his lighter weight allowed him to sprint at high speeds and climb any tree with ease, perfect for hunting. They were also waiting for Gurath, the village's local storyteller, to tell one of his famous stories.

The crowd grew silent as a man stepped into the storytelling circle. Many soon realized with disappointment that this was not Gurath, but a different man entirely. He spoke in a quivering tone, "Gurath apologizes for not being able to make it to this wonderful festival. A personal matter arose, and he had to travel to Bootskin. Again, he wishes you will all forgive him and hopes that the rest of the festival will be enjoyable. Thank you." The man bowed and then hastily left. Several people booed at the news; Gurath was the only reason they had come.

Banju, Rik and Terin left soon after and began to walk home. "Pity Gurath couldn't make it," Banju said. Aside from his father, Gurath was the most influential person in Banju's life.

Terin nodded. "Aye. I fancy his stories; the fantasies within them send my imagination to different realms."

"You mean you don't believe any of his stories are true?" Rik seemed surprised by this.

"No," Terin stated, "I don't. Elves, dwarves and Drifters haven't been seen or heard from in hundreds of years, so how do we know that they existed in the first place? What if the Eradication never really took place? Where's the proof to back up his stories? There isn't much!"

Banju patiently glanced up at the shining moon as he thought of the best response. "Sometimes things don't need definitive proof. If I told you your house burned down while you were in a different town, would you believe me?"

"Probably," Terin conceded.

"Why? You haven't seen your house, so currently there's no proof, and yet you believe it has burned down simply because I told you it has."

Terin sighed. "You're right, Banju, not everything needs proof. But I still don't believe in fairy tales."

They stopped walking, for they were outside the Arrow's Hammer, Thanju's well-known blacksmith shop. They said their farewells, and Banju opened the door to their home; the temperature drastically rose. There was a sound of metal hitting metal: the welcoming sound of home. They put their satchels on a hanger by the door and continued on to the kitchen, a dimly lit room with almost an entire wall of windows looking out into the manicured garden.

The hammering stopped abruptly, and the door to the forge—located right by the kitchen—opened and their father Thanju stepped in, wiping his dirty hands with a clean rag. Not a better blacksmith could be found in all the northern regions; or the entire kingdom, for that matter.

Errands, Stories and Farewells

Thanju nodded his head toward them. "How was the festival? Did Gurath tell one of his famous stories again?" Thanju was tall and muscular, his rough, scarred skin hidden beneath a black beard. His brown, welcoming eyes gentled his tough demeanor and always encouraged the boys to tell him the truth.

"Not this time," Banju answered, "he was away on business."

Thanju tilted his head thoughtfully. "It must have been important for him to miss the festival. Well, there's always next year, I suppose!"

Their father moved to the organized counter in the kitchen and grabbed an apple from a basket. He gestured with the apple toward his sons, they nodded, and he tossed both of them one. Thunder rumbled outside, and Thanju glanced out a nearby window to look at the approaching storm. "That's the crazy thing about living here: It's warm some days and then others it's cold and rainy for weeks on end. Autumn seems to be a year-round ordeal."

They all took a seat at the kitchen table and enjoyed their savory apples. Once they finished, Thanju said to Rik, "Sorry, Rik, I was going to make your favorite meal tonight, but Boro's Concoction is going to have to wait until tomorrow."

Rik shrugged. "I suppose I can wait another day."

"Ah, speaking of tomorrow, I'm going to need your help," Thanju directed this at Banju, "I have to deliver a selection of fine weaponry and armor to Duke Maltren."

Banju perked up. Duke Maltren was one of the richest individuals in the village, second only to the governor himself. No one knew why he settled in Smith Village, though many theorized it was for the peace and quiet. Regardless, his wealth and title had provided him with a wide array of friends and a house worthy of a king. Banju had always wondered what it looked like inside, and he would soon find out.

After setting up plans for the coming errand, they all retired for the night. On the morn they hastily ate breakfast, packed the delivery and headed on their way. The Duke's estate was located on the other side of town; they had quite a walk ahead.

Several passersby acknowledged them; in Smith Village, everyone knew everyone; to an extent, at least. When your father was the best smith in the village, it was even harder to go unnoticed.

To pass the time, Thanju began to whistle.

"What tune is that, father?" Banju asked.

"This, my boy, was a folksong of Quinsael." Thanju whistled a moment longer before continuing, "Your mother and I used to dance to it all the time."

"You lived in Quinsael?" Banju asked as casually as he could; his father's history was a touchy subject, especially when it involved his mother.

"Aye," his father replied solemnly, "we lived there before it was attacked and destroyed. Quaint town, it was. Smaller than this one, and more peaceful if you can believe it." A smile crossed his face. "'Twas where you and Rik were born!"

"Why was it destroyed?"

Silence fell. "For savage reasons, as all unnecessary destruction is. We were lucky enough to leave before it fell."

It was common knowledge that Quinsael had fallen sixteen years earlier. Banju couldn't help himself. "How soon before?"

Thanju chuckled. "Why the sudden interest?"

"I'm just curious because you've never mentioned it before."

Silence fell again, this time lifted by a sigh. "I suppose you deserve to know," his father conceded. "After all, I've kept you in the dark for sixteen years." Banju's breath caught in his lungs as his anticipation intensified. "Quinsael was raided while we still lived there, but we escaped."

Banju's anticipation collapsed. "That's it?"

"What were you expecting, a heroic tale filled with action and adventure?" his father asked humorously.

"Actually, yes." Banju regretted the words the moment that he said them, but now he was past the point of no return. "I know that there is more to the story, and I understand that there are some things that you don't want to tell us, but please stop beating around the bush every time we ask you a question about your past!" His voice came out harsher than he had expected.

"There are indeed things that I have kept from you." His father spoke barely above a whisper, stinging Banju more than if he had yelled. "But I have just reasons, Banju. You need to understand that."

"What reasons?" Banju persisted.

"Love. I bear a heavy burden, and I do not wish to share it with you and Rik. I promise that I will reveal all to you when the time comes. But that time is not now."

His fighting spirit gone, Banju began, "I'm sorry, f—"

"There is nothing to apologize for, my son."

Silence enveloped them again and did not alleviate until they arrived at Duke Maltren's estate. The house was unlike any other in sheer size, design or architecture. It was made entirely out of bricks, a rarity in a village filled with huts and cabins. Three stories tall, the house dwarfed all others. Plants hung from its two balconies, and a wide marble archway led to the estate's door.

Thanju knocked, and a servant soon answered. "Can I help you, gentlemen?"

"We are here to deliver the weapons and armor Duke Maltren requested," Thanju replied.

"Of course. Right this way." They followed the servant up a flight of stairs, through a long corridor decorated with rich tapestries and to another corridor bare of any decoration. "This is where I must stop. At the end of this corridor, there is a door that will lead you directly to the Duke's quarters."

The servant then bowed his head and left, and they continued on their own until they reached the door. "Banju, give me your satchel."

"Why?"

His father held out his hand for emphasis. "I must speak to the Duke alone. Head back to the entrance, and I will meet you there once I have finished."

Banju reluctantly did as he was told; he had been looking forward to meeting the Duke. He retraced their steps and waited patiently by the entrance. He admired the several boar, deer, moose and bear mounts on the walls. That, however, only kept him occupied for a few moments. He said hello to a passing servant and then began to pace. A few girls Banju's age headed for the entrance but stopped when they saw him pacing there. He also stopped, raised his hand in an effort to wave and was only able to let out a brief "Hi" before nervousness overtook him. The girls giggled and walked out the door.

In all his sixteen years at Smith Village, he had not had one real relationship with a girl. Not for lack of trying—it was mostly because his heart found no match in the masses of the village. "There's plenty o' fish in the sea," fishermen from Dunar always quoted. Banju resumed his pacing.

Minutes passed, and eventually his curiosity overcame his better judgment; he *had* to know why his father was talking with the Duke. Banju cautiously made his way back to the hallway leading to the Duke's chamber and placed his ear on the door.

"…many are going to die," the Duke was saying, "I suggest we tread carefully."

"It is not us who need to be careful, but the king himself," Banju's father replied. "Depending on how he handles the situation, he could end up destroying his life along with the rest of Shallor."

"Aye, King Banton has been known to make rash decisions from time to time. Surely there is something we can do?"

"We cannot; we would be meddling in affairs beyond our control. The repercussions would be devastating."

"More devastating than letting events happen unchecked?"

"Perhaps. How is our border looking?"

"My officers have informed me that there has been no activity, just as there has been none for two hundred years. The Korethan Barrier has kept them contained. However, there is one place where they could slip through."

"The gate separating them from Shallor."

"Precisely. It has not been opened for two centuries, but if it does, my men may not be able to hold them off."

"There is also a possibility that they have dug tunnels to sneak into Shallor. Is Fayn still their leader?"

"We do not know. Certainly there is no way that he could still be alive."

"Anything is possible in this magical land; if only everyone would remember and accept that."

"Aye. Perhaps they will realize it again someday soon."

"If not in our lifetime, then in the next. I must be going; Banju is most likely wondering what is keeping me."

Footsteps approached the door, and Banju sprinted back to the entranceway before his father could discover that he had eavesdropped. He pretended to be observing one of the Duke's tapestries as his father returned. "You ready to leave, Banju?" Thanju asked, no hint of suspicion in his voice.

"Hmm? Oh, yes." Banju stumbled out the door and followed his father, musing over the implications of what he had heard. He had known that his father was hiding something for quite some time, but never suspected it to be something like this.

Not a word was spoken between them on their way home, and it was not long before Thanju began to have suspicions of his own. However, once they entered their home, they soon disregarded these thoughts in place of happier, more optimistic ones. Gurath had been invited for dinner, and the house needed to be prepared. Banju cleaned the study, dusting the books and removing the ashes from the fireplace while Rik swept the floor and his father began to cut the raw beef for Boro's Concoction. The table was set with their best glasses, plates and silverware, and a few logs were put on the fire to set it ablaze. Within the late afternoon when Gurath arrived, the house was ready.

"Gurath, my friend," Thanju said with a smile, "the boys tell me you were not at the festival last night. What kept you, if you don't mind me asking?"

Gurath sighed and sat down in a plush chair by the fire. He was an elderly gentleman who had seen better days, but his tall, strong-built figure indicated years of hard work and exercise. His gentle eyes were hidden by a gold beard and hair with scattered gray. Over the years, his graceful and gentle demeanor— along with his immense knowledge and wisdom—had gained him the respect of everyone in the village and the surrounding area. "My niece in Bootskin had a son, and they requested I visit," he answered in his smooth, knowing voice. "I preferred to stay, but she's the only family I have left."

"We understand." Thanju moved back into the kitchen. "Perhaps you could make it up to the boys by telling them one of your stories while I finish preparing our supper."

Gurath made himself comfortable in the chair and gazed patiently at Banju and Rik. "Very well. Which story would you like to hear?"

"Any story would be fine, sir," Rik said respectfully, hiding his excitement.

"Tell them the one about the end of the Golden Age," Thanju suggested from the kitchen.

When the boys did not object, Gurath cleared his throat and began, a solemn look in his eyes, "This story, like nearly all I tell, is less a tale and more a recounting of forgotten times. It would be best for the two of you to heed what I say and take note of the mistakes of the past. Long ago, the Great King Sagaxus, who ruled Shallor at the time, discovered that the people of the desolate land of Makir were planning to attack and conquer Shallor." Banju and Rik perked up, for Sagaxus was known to be one of the greatest warriors and leaders in Shallor's history, and Makir was Shallor's sworn enemy. "When he received this news, Sagaxus sprang into action, rallying men, elves, dwarves and Drifters to his side.

"Narkk, the king of Makir, had stolen one of the most powerful weapons in history from Shallor: the Golden Gauntlet, a mystical object that had the ability to create anything of nature. Trees, animals, creatures; you name it, and he could create it. However, when it was first created, the elves and dwarves restricted it from being able to create man; a skill, they deemed, that should only belong to the

Creator himself. Narkk and Sagaxus believed that the Gauntlet was the key to winning the war.

"Sagaxus and his men waged a great battle against Narkk and his forces of darkness in the valley outside of Narkk's castle. When it appeared as if Sagaxus's men would triumph, Narkk brought out the Gauntlet, killing many legions. Seeing this, Sagaxus charged toward Narkk with a group of elite warriors, and an epic duel ensued. The elite warriors fell quickly, but Sagaxus would not admit defeat. As he was about to deliver a death blow, Narkk created fire with the Gauntlet and disintegrated Sagaxus into ashes." At this, he looked into the flames of the fireplace, and the boys could almost see the final battle taking place in its embers. "But Narkk would soon realize what a huge mistake that was; his foul play enraged all of Sagaxus's army and they all charged him at once. He held his ground for a short time before they overran and killed him.

"This would mark the end of Makir's reign of terror, but also the end of the Great King's peaceful kingdom. A fact often left out is that his best friend took Sagaxus's only son to a secret sanctuary; he had sworn to Sagaxus that he would protect his son until the end of time itself.

"Back in Shallor, many began to believe that magic should be purged from the land since it was magic that had killed the greatest leader in history. Leron used this to his advantage and briefly became the new king." He stopped briefly, as if saddened by what he was about to say next. "The Eradication of Magic began. Man went insane, executing every magician, elf, witch, Drifter or anyone else associated with magic that they could get their hands on. Not one of them was left alive. Faith was lost, and dark days began.

"To this day, the Golden Gauntlet, the very catalyst to the Eradication, has not been rediscovered; however, many believe that it is buried somewhere beneath the ashes of the battlefield in Makir, in the exact place that Narkk was killed." Gurath cleared his throat again and laid back further into the chair. "That is all I have to say, though there are many tales that led up to and followed these events. Do you have any questions?"

Banju and Rik were speechless, letting settle all that they had heard. Not a noise was uttered, save the clattering of pots as their father continued cooking. Finally, Banju recovered enough to ask, "I know you've explained what they are before, but I've forgotten. What was a Drifter?"

"That is a story in and of itself, one that could go on for days. I will try to give you a brief description so as not to lecture you into boredom." Gurath steepled his fingers. "Drifters existed long before a kingdom was established in Shallor. They were law keepers, righting wrongs, aiding the helpless and protecting the land, even if that meant protecting Shallor from itself. As the years went on, they developed special abilities. Magical abilities. Each

Drifter had a power unlike the others, but all were given the same base attributes: long life, and the capability to 'drift' ten feet off the ground for extended periods of time. Eventually they acquired steeds greater than horses: dragons, griffins and the like. Sadly, they met their end along with all of the other magic users during the Eradication. I apologize if this description is too brief and open-ended; it's the best I could think of without going into vivid detail."

Banju thanked him, amazed.

Their father soon announced that dinner was ready, and they all migrated to the kitchen table. Boro's Concoction was not only Rik's favorite, but also a favorite amongst all his friends and family. Soft egg noodles layered with tender beef and a thick, creamy sauce entered their mouths. They all ate until their stomachs could hold no more, and then they forced down another serving. Once they had finished, they pushed aside their plates and allowed the food to digest.

"Do you remember when we first met, Gurath?" Thanju asked with a wide grin.

Gurath returned his smile. "Who could forget?" He glanced at the boys. "Your father had just arrived in Smith Village and was looking for a place to stay. To his chagrin, all of the inns were full."

"We came to Smith Village around this time of the year," Thanju added.

"Your father, with all of his patience, desperately searched for a place to rest his head. He found it, but not the way a normal man would."

"At that time this house belonged to…" Thanju waved his hand, "to someone whose name does not matter."

Gurath chuckled. "The resident was a reckless man and oftentimes drunk. He offered your father a deal: he would give your father the house and all of its possessions if he would face the drunkard in a duel. Initially, your father refused, but—"

"—but Gurath approached me and informed me that this man was no duelist, only a prideful pretender. So I agreed to the fool's terms."

"It was a duel worthy of songs."

"If you can call me tripping a man into defeat worthy," Thanju laughed.

Gurath and the boys joined in, their faces turning red and their eyes filling with mirthful tears. Once the laughing subsided, Gurath said, "Though this has been pleasant, I really must be going; the sun has set, a storm is nearly upon us and my old bones call me to slumber." He bade farewell and embarked on his walk home.

Thanju, Banju and Rik sat for a few moments longer before Thanju stirred. "Rik, I'm sure you've been wondering why tonight was such a special occasion. You turned seventeen last week; I think it's time for me to give you permission to do what you've wanted to do for years."

Rik straightened in his seat. "You mean…"

Thanju nodded. "You have my permission to leave this household and travel across Shallor to your heart's desire."

"Really? No Joke?"

Thanju's face broke into a smile. "No joke. You can go whenever you want."

"Can I leave tomorrow?"

Thanju leaned closer. "You'd better start packing."

Rik's seat fell over as he ran to his room. Thanju and Banju chuckled as they watched him go. "You know, Banju, you can still leave home whenever you see fit," his father said, a hint of hope in his voice.

Banju nodded. "I know, father, but my place is here with you and this shop."

"We both know that you want to do more than just stay here for the rest of your life forging things with metal."

"Yes, and we also both know that the law states that peasants can't become knights, so thus you're stuck with me."

"Unless you become a squire," Thanju pointed out.

"I am too old for squiring; knighthood is not worth it if I become one with half of my years gone."

With that, they sat in silence as they listened to Rik packing, the rain pattering against the roof and the thunder rumbling. Each time the thunder roared,

Banju noted that his father's face became more and more depressed.

"What's the matter, father?" he asked with concern.

Thanju looked up at Banju as if he had just woken from a bad dream. There was a pause, and the thunder rumbled again. "Nothing, son; just remembering something, is all."

Banju nodded as if he understood and stood up. "I'm going to go see if Rik needs any help packing."

As he walked away, Thanju broke out of his trance and watched Banju leave. "You deserve to be a knight," he murmured.

Rik was just beginning to put things in his satchel when Banju entered his room. "Need any help?"

Rik habitually gripped the seven-inch long hilt of his custom built two-and-a-half-foot-long sword. "No, I don't think so, but you can keep me company."

Banju almost laughed at how hastily Rik was packing, but he suppressed it in time to ask, "Where do you think you'll go?"

Rik shrugged as he put more clothing in the satchel. "Maybe Elk Village; definitely not Cebil or Aldor, those cities are *too* big. However, I might brave the shore and city life and get a job at Dunar."

"Or you could go to Bāes Lark and live with ghosts the rest of your life," Banju joked.

Rik smiled and put his life earnings of coins in a small sack. They stayed up for hours that night, reliving old memories, talking about the future and enjoying their last few moments together. Tomorrow would be the beginning of a change, a change that would set their destinies into motion.

The Dark Horizon

When Banju finally fell asleep that night, he had one of the worst dreams of his life:

He saw his father riding on a horse in a forest during a terrible thunderstorm, holding a young Banju in one arm and a baby Rik in the other. No words could be heard, but it was clear that they were running from something. Lightning flashed; Banju was now his present age, racing in a dark haze to his father's blacksmith shop.

His father was fighting a man garbed in a black cloak, calling Banju to come help defeat the stranger, but Banju could not move. He watched helplessly as his father was stabbed and fell to the ground.

The dream ended with a man with an ugly scar on the left side of his face looking at Banju and saying,

"Come to me, you belong to me, come to me." *Banju began to walk to him, and the man smiled, raised his sword and brought it down on Banju.*

Banju woke to the deep rumble of thunder. He noticed that he was gasping and sweating. *That was weird,* he thought.

He sat in his bed until he heard Rik walk into the kitchen. "Good morning," Rik said when Banju followed suit.

"If you can call it a morning," Banju remarked. The thunderstorm seemed to still be going on as if it had just begun.

"I've been listening to the storm for awhile now," Rik informed him. "It's almost done."

"Counting the seconds between each rumble of thunder?"

Rik nodded with a smile, and then his face grew grim. "As soon as father wakes, I'm leaving."

Banju put his hand on Rik's shoulder. "I'll miss you."

"I'll miss you, too."

Just then Thanju groggily stepped into the room. "Are you heading off?"

"Once I grab my things," Rik replied.

Thanju held up a finger. "I'll be right back." He returned with a small bag and a durable looking walking stick and handed them to Rik. "The bag is full of gold coins, and the walking stick I crafted myself. It's not much, but these should help your journey go a little more smoothly."

Rik took the gifts and hugged his father. "Thank you, father."

"I love you, son; be safe." Thanju began to shed tears.

"I love you, too, father, and I will try my best."

It took another half an hour for them to say their final farewells, and then Banju and Rik headed for the east gate out of the village.

The storm had stopped, but the sky was still covered in dark, wispy clouds, and the air was cold and brisk. There were few people out on the streets aside from those beginning to open their shops and others seemingly walking around with no apparent objective in mind.

The three-meter tall eastern gate came too soon for Banju and Rik. Banju looked beyond the gate, at the winding dirt path that went all the way to the Smith Mountains and beyond. He followed Rik out of the gate a few steps, and then they both stopped. After a moment's silence, they embraced in a long bear hug. They parted, both on the brink of tears, and Banju watched on in sadness as Rik rode his horse down the path into his yet unknown future.

Once Rik was only a small speck in the distance, Banju turned to go home, but stopped when he saw an old gray bearded man being dragged out of the village by two guards. The man wore torn clothes and looked like he had lived a very rough life. An odd black scar spiraled around his right palm and up his arm.

"Please, put me down!" The man exclaimed, yet he did not seem angry that he was being dragged out of the village by the guards; he seemed calm and collected. "I can at least walk myself out from here."

The guards hesitantly put him down, and the man staggered out of the gate.

Banju felt compelled to go to the man and help him. "Are you alright, sir?"

The man did not seem the least bit surprised at somebody coming to his aid. "Oh, I'm fine, thank you."

"Please, come home with me and I'll give you some clean clothes and warm food to eat," Banju insisted.

The man held up a hand, revealing his black scar once more. "No, no, I'll be fine." He looked up at the clouded sky and his face turned grim. "Besides, something bad is about to happen in Smith Village and I'm glad that they threw me out before it happens."

"What's going to happen?"

The man stopped, still glancing at the darkened sky. His gray eyes were deep and crestfallen, as if he had glimpsed everything in the world around him and did not like what he had seen. "Evil has entered Shallor again, lots of evil. Evil has gathered its forces in many places and is plotting to take over Shallor, and it will triumph. A storm is brewing on the dark horizon, and it will not abate until it has consumed us all." He looked at Banju as if seeing him for the first time. "But you, you will play an important role in saving Shallor." He placed his scarred hand on Banju's shoulder, and a huge burst of energy filled Banju's body. "You, Banju, will face much despair and many challenges, but you will be the key to our victory.

"H-how did you know my name?" Banju silently gasped at the amount of energy flowing through him.

As the man removed his hand, the energy boost left Banju. "Because I know things you can't possibly comprehend." He turned and began to walk down the path. "Return home, Banju, and destiny will find you."

Banju stood, unable to speak, unable to move, as the mysterious man walked away, no longer staggering, but striding with power and purpose as he disappeared into fog.

It took Banju another few minutes to regain the ability to walk and even longer to remember that he could think and speak. *Who was that man?* He wondered as he walked back to the gate.

"Excuse me, do you know who that bearded man was who was just thrown out of the village?" he asked one of the guards.

"Don't know 'is name, but 'e was in a bar tellin' people their fates." The guard forced a smile. "Not many people liked what 'e 'ad to say, so they threw 'im out."

With that, Banju began to walk home. He was almost there when he noticed a new announcement on the wall outside of town hall. It read:

His Royal Highness, King Banton III, decrees:

Any eligible man, be he peasant or noble, who wishes to tryout for knighthood, may travel to Aldor immediately. Those who make it through the tryouts will join the king's army and have the opportunity to become a knight. The tryouts will be held in Aldor in eleven days.

After he read it, Banju returned home to see if his father had heard, but his father was nowhere to be found.

While he was waiting, Banju went into the forge and sharpened and polished several arrows, axes and swords. He was just finishing the last sword when he heard his father walk into the house.

Thanju was carrying a bag full of fruits, vegetables and bread, indicating that he had gone to the marketplace. "Did you see the king's message?"

Banju nodded. "I did."

"Well, are you going to go?"

"I already told you: My place is here with you and the forge."

"What's holding you back?"

Nothing, Banju wanted to say, *I just don't want to lose you like I have lost mother and Rik.*

His father shrugged. "Very well, if that's what you want. I suppose that since you're staying you can make your famous vegetable stew tonight." He began to leave the room, but stopped halfway there. "But if you happen to change your mind, and I hope you do, you're welcome to go. You would make a fine knight, Banju."

"Alright, father." Ignoring his father's last statement, Banju began to gather the vegetables he would need for the stew.

○○○

Rik's Trek

Rik glanced behind him and saw that Smith Village was nothing but a small dot across the wide horizon. Sadness and victory filled him as he realized that he was finally leaving the only place he had known since birth. Now he was heading into the great unknown, unsure of its gifts and challenges.

From the dirt path he trod, Rik could see the Smith Mountains looming on his left. To his right he could see a distant forest and the tips of the mountains that surrounded the Citadel of Shallor. He wished that it were summer so that the grass around him would be a lush green instead of the dead brown flanking him.

He noticed a path heading for the mountains and considered it; only one civilized town existed in the mountains, but Rik suspected that it would not be an ideal place to live. Visit, maybe, but never stay there. Pass Town was always rumored to be the most underdeveloped place in the entire kingdom. Many believed it was so backward because it was cut off from the rest of humanity and the journey up to it was perilous due to bandits, narrow paths, sudden drops and savage animals. Some even believed the narrow passes to still be inhabited by fearsome mythological creatures.

No, he decided, *I will not go there… just yet.*

As Rik deliberated, he remembered an old saying,

> There is a path,
> A winding path,
> That takes me where I need to go.
> This path,
> This winding path,
> Takes me places I do not yet know.

So where was this path taking him? There was also Elk Village, but Rik was not so sure about that, either. It had everything he wanted: shade, peace, hunting and the like. The problem was that it was just a step up from Smith Village and he would probably never make a name for himself there. He wanted to go down in the history books as someone who had done something important, not as someone who had lived out his life hunting the biggest game in the forest.

I could always go to Aldor and try out to be a knight, he thought with amusement. He had heard traders talking about it before he had left. At that time, he had thought it best not to tell Banju. Besides, it would only be a matter of time before the message reached Smith Village.

What else could he do besides become a knight? There was Dunar, which was established right by the great sea, something that Rik had never seen before. He did not know of anything he could do there besides perhaps take up a job as a watchman. A boring job, for sure, but if he did it long enough he could be promoted to something of higher importance. If that did not work out, he could always become a sailor or find work elsewhere; it was a huge, bustling city, after all.

Yes, that would be where he would go; now he just had to get there. He knew that it was at least three hundred miles away, if not more. *I feel sorry for my horse.* His horse's hooves were beginning to tread heavily and he knew that soon they would need to stop for a break. A lone giant apple tree stood out just ahead and he resolved that that would be an ideal place to sit.

He picked an apple for the horse and himself and sat with his back resting on the tree's trunk. The apple was one of the best apples he had had in a long time: it sent energy back into Rik's body as if he had never even begun his journey and was still fully rested back home. He thought it was odd that he felt this way, but figured it was because he had not had anything to eat for several hours and his body was just giving the illusion of being fully rejuvenated. But if this feeling was for real…

It could not be, for there was no such thing as a re-energizing apple. He laughed at this crazy idea and happily chewed on it. *I wish that there were some way that we could reach Dunar quickly without getting exhausted.*

Just then, he heard the gentle pounding of horses' hooves and saw two horses pulling a wagon approaching the tree. The wagon stopped in front of him and an old man leaped out and walked toward him. The man looked muscular and had a confident air about him.

"Do you need some assistance, sir?" he asked Rik. "I was just on my way to deliver some supplies to Dunar when I noticed you sitting under this tree."

Rik was speechless at first, but came to his senses when he realized the opportunity that had just sprung up. "Um…Um yes, I was heading there, too."

"Well you can hitch a ride with me if you'd like, sir."

He took another bite of the apple and gulped. This was too good to be true; what if the man was a bandit or kidnapper? "Are you sure?"

The man nodded and smiled. "Yes, of course I am! However, the decision is completely up to you." He got back into his wagon and grabbed the horses' reins.

Rik briefly thought about it and then shrugged. "I'll go with you."

"Very well; hop in the back an' make sure no bandits steal my supplies! You can tie your horse to the back so that it may rest."

Rik did as he said.

They set off, and Rik was soon tremendously glad that he had made this decision. At the rate they were going, he estimated they would reach the city in no time. *Farewell, Smith Village; hello, Dunar!*

○ ○ ○

Tragedy

The next day, two guards were standing outside the western gate of Smith Village.

"This job is pointless," one of the guards complained to the other. "No one ever comes in or leaves through the western gate!"

"Actually," the other guard said cheerfully, "we go through it all the time!"

The first guard was about to scold his friend for such a dumb remark but then thought better of it when he saw the frightened look on the other's face. "What's wrong?"

The other guard gulped and pointed down the path. "S-somebody's comin' to the gate!"

The first guard looked where his friend was pointing and saw a dark cloaked figure on the horizon. He looked back at the high stone wall and said, "What's that guy doing over here? There's nothing in the western region except marshland and rifts!"

"Perhaps he's lost," the other guard suggested, the cheerful tone in his voice gone. "Or he could be a criminal, or worse, an omen, like the ones we've heard about in stories."

"I say we block his path until we find out who he is; no use bein' careless."

"Agreed."

When the cloaked figure approached the gate, the two guards blocked the entrance by forming an "x" with their pikes. A black mask could be seen under the shadow of the cloaked figure's hood. "Halt!" the first guard ordered. "State your name and business here in Smith Village."

The voice that replied sent chills down their backs. "I go by many names, but I am no one of consequence to you," it hissed in a deep, unearthly tone.

"That's not a good answer! Pull back your cowl and reveal your face now, or turn around and go back to wherever you came from!"

The cloaked figure let out a hoarse laugh. "You are too cowardly to see my face!" Before the guards could reply, there was a sound like a blade leaving its sheath, and the guards were decapitated in an instant. The four spikes quickly retracted back into the stranger's right hand. "Thank you for allowing me entrance, gentlemen; I have a job to finish."

Elsewhere, Banju and Terin went out of Smith Village into the woods to spar with wooden swords. Certainly, they owned real swords, but this had long ago become their tradition; in many ways, it was the only way they could communicate with each other.

"Are you ready, Banju?" Terin spun his weapon and held it low to the ground.

Banju took a defensive pose. "Are you?"

Without answering, Terin rushed toward Banju, sword upraised. "So are you going to go to Aldor?"

Banju blocked the attack and stepped back. "I haven't decided yet." He blocked a blow to the side. "What about you?"

"Well, I think I'm only going to go if you are, considering I don't know anyone over there." He tried to strike Banju again, but to no avail. "I wonder where we would go after training. Some people are saying the king is increasing the army because he plans to attack Makir."

Banju swung his sword, just missing Terin's shoulder. "Well, that could be it."

"That would be something," Terin said thoughtfully and did a hit combo, which was blocked every time. "After all the stories we've heard about Makir, it would be interesting to actually be there and see where the stories took place."

"Ah, so you *do* believe the stories are true?" Banju did a twirling attack to no gain.

Terin shrugged and feigned for Banju's left and tried to strike Banju's right, but was blocked. "Maybe just a little."

They sparred for another hour with neither one of them striking an imaginary deathblow to the other. Afterward, they sat up high in an oak tree, gulping down water.

"So how's business at the Arrow's Hammer?" Terin asked.

Banju moved his legs into a more comfortable position. "It's going great: more and more people seem to be realizing that my father is one of the best blacksmiths in this region."

"That's good."

"How's your father's hunting supply store doing?"

This was usually a touchy subject, for it was well known that Terin and his father had a strained relationship, but he replied, "We've had a few ups and downs with some customers, but overall it's going well. One man recently came in and asked us if we had anything for Minotaurs." He laughed. "It took nearly an hour to explain to him that they've been extinct for a while now."

"What about that report ten years ago of a Minotaur attacking a campsite?"

"Funny, he brought that up." Terin threw a dead branch and watched it soar over the autumn trees. "We told him that that may be the only exception, if it wasn't really a prank gone wrong. Later, a woman asked for our biggest bow. Apparently a deer had tackled her while she was riding."

"Is that even possible?"

"Apparently."

They talked for another few hours, exchanging stories, watching the wildlife passing by below and enjoying the peace that only nature could give them.

"Do you remember when we were little how we used to pretend that dead tree over there a terrifying beast?" Terin asked with a chuckle.

Banju smiled. "Aye, I remember. We were, what, six, seven? I would keep its tentacles occupied in the front while you would sneak up from behind for the finishing kill."

"But it was smarter than that…"

"…it would knock you to the ground and I would try to save you, but it would wrap me in its unforgiving grasp…"

"…then I would roll over, cut off a few of its tentacles…"

"…and save me before it could eat me."

They both burst out laughing. "Those were the days," Terin said.

"Indeed they were."

Suddenly the sun was covered by dark storm clouds; the wind became stronger and colder, causing the colored leaves of the trees to swirl around the woods like a tornado. When this happened, Banju felt something calling him, telling him to go home immediately. "I think I should go home; it's getting late."

Terin got his bow out. "I'm going to stay up here and see if I can't bring back some game."

"Alright, see you later." Banju reached the bottom of the tree and began to run quickly toward the northern gate of Smith Village. He heard a twig snap behind him and looked to see what it was. "Terin?" There was no reply. Slightly shaken, he ran even faster.

As he hammered bent metal into submission, Thanju cheerfully whistled the song he had danced with Elaine to back in Quinsael. The king had recently requested a large order of weaponry, and Thanju was happy to oblige. *Just seventy-nine more swords to go.*

He was just cooling metal to make another when he heard a knock on the door. "Banju, are you home already?" He wiped his hands off and slowly headed for the door when it was knocked on again. "Be patient; I'm coming!"

As if in response, the door flew from its hinges as a dark cloaked figure entered.

Thanju stopped in his tracks and gasped, memories of the past painfully returning. "You!"

The figure tilted its head. "Thought you killed me, didn't you? You will soon discover that I cannot be killed so easily. You and I," there was a sound like the unsheathing of a sword and spikes slowly drew out of its knuckles, "have a battle to finish."

There was a red flash, and a sword appeared in Thanju's hand. "And so we do."

Banju was stopped abruptly when a guard halted him outside the gate. "What's your business here, sir?"

"I live here!" Banju exclaimed.

"Please state your name."

"My name is Banju, son of Thanju. Perhaps you've heard of him? He owns a blacksmith shop called the Arrow's Hammer."

"Okay, just had to make sure, 'cause we just found two dead guards outside the western gate." The guard stepped aside and waved his hand. "Go ahead."

Banju dashed home, but stopped when he saw that the front door had been ripped from its frame. He walked cautiously into the house, hunting knife in hand.

There were signs that a battle had been fought: the walls had been scraped by blades, glass lay shattered on the floor and the table and a few chairs had been reduced to splinters.

Banju methodically checked each room for his father. "Father, are you here?"

He heard coughing and a muffled, "Banju…"

Banju walked into his father's study and found his father lying on the floor, four gaping bloody punctures in his chest.

"Father!" Banju rushed to his father's side. "What happened?" He grabbed a rag from the desk and put it on Thanju's wounds to try to stop the bleeding.

His father looked up at him. "Is…is he still here?"

"I'm the only one here."

Thanju's breathing became ragged. He pointed to one of the bookcases in the study. "Top of the bookcase…furthest right…take the book…and keep what's inside."

"Come on; let's get you to a doctor."

Thanju slowly shook his head. "It's too late for that now, son. The poison has already begun to take effect." He gripped Banju's hand. "Never give up, Banju, whatever you do, don't give up."

Tears flowed down Banju's cheeks. "No, father, don't leave me! I need you! Who did this to you?"

His father looked him straight in the eyes. "Things may seem hopeless now, but all you need do is find bird's resting place…"

"What does that mean?"

"I love you, son…" Thanju closed his eyes and drifted into the quiet and peaceful sleep of death.

Banju cradled his father in his arms and raised his head and bellowed a long, painful, continuous scream.

A week later, Banju stood by his father's grave. The funeral had gone smoothly; nearly the entire village had shown up, but Banju did not feel right being the only family member there since no one knew where Rik had gone.

Gurath put his hand on Banju's shoulder. "Your father was a good man and a friend to us all, Banju. If you ever need anything, I'm only a request away."

Banju tried to smile, but failed. "Thank you, Gurath, that means a lot to me."

As Gurath left, Terin approached, the air cold enough to see his breath. "I'm truly sorry, Banju." He embraced Banju and then stood at his side. "Do you know who did it?"

"No, but I'm going to find out."

They were now the only people in the graveyard, and it began to lightly snow.

"So what are you going to do now?" Terin asked.

Banju looked up at the gray sky and the falling snow. He felt empty and hopeless, as if there was nothing left in the world worth fighting for...*No,* he thought flatly, *there* is *something to fight for.* "For seven days I have eaten alone, hearing every noise, every creak, every howl of the wind and yearning for the silence to be filled with my father's voice. There is nothing left for me here, besides the blacksmith shop, and right now that is nearly too painful to enter. I'm going to travel to Aldor, pass the tryouts, do what the king wants and then I'm going to find my father's killer and pay him back wound for wound."

"Then we go together."

The Journey

The next day as Banju packed, his eyes drifted to the bookcase. "Top shelf, furthest right," Banju said aloud. He scanned the top shelf and saw that it was occupied by a thick, unmarked tome. Oddly, when he pulled it off the shelf, there was a clicking noise. *What could that be?* Banju felt around where the tome had been and found a small lever embedded in the shelf. He pulled it toward him and immediately stepped back, for the entire bookcase had sunk into the wall and moved to the left, revealing a chamber within.

Mystified, he stepped down a short flight of stairs and into the hidden room. It was a small, circular room with a sword hanging on one side and a chest and a table topped with different types of documents on the other. Blue and yellow glowing rocks implanted in the ceiling lit the scene.

The sword drew Banju's attention the most, so he approached it and retrieved it off the wall by its hilt. It was a cross hilt, black with silver wiring wrapped around it. The cross section was silver and the sword blade was three and a half feet long. The sheath was black, and toward the top of the sheath the word "*Crikkon*" was inlaid in golden letters. He drew it with a satisfying *swish* and was amazed at how balanced and perfect it felt in his hand. The blade's main color was silver, but when it was turned at certain angles, it was possible to see shimmering streaks of gold and blue.

He sheathed it and moved toward the chest, which he noticed had a note on its top.

Banju,

If you are reading this, then my past has finally caught up with me. I wish I could be with you now, son, but be comforted that we will see each other again. Remember everything I have taught you and you will be able to face any challenge. This sword saved me during many skirmishes in my day, and now I pass it on to you. Everything inside the house, the house itself, the stable, the land and the shop now belong to you and Rik. Choose wisely what you do with it all.

Your beloved father,
Thanju

Banju smiled briefly, closed the letter and tied his new sword Crikkon to his belt. This sword, he knew, was only the beginning of a new change within him. Now to see what was in the chest. He nearly fainted when he opened it; it was filled to the brim with gold coins and jewels of every shape, size and color. As he sat gaping at the spectacle, he wondered how it was possible for his father to have been so rich without them even knowing. *Perhaps one of these documents will explain things.*

In a way, they did. Many turned out to be treasure maps with notes scribbled all over them. However, one thing on the table turned out not to be a scroll or piece of paper at all, but rather a full-length book. He opened it, recognized his father's handwriting and began to read.

It has been a tough couple of days. I guess that can be expected when you live on an island ruled by barbarians. Burdick and I have decided that we will be leaving in a few days. He found a treasure map and believes it will lead us to enough treasure to live peacefully and safe from the ones hunting us. I could care less; I'm just ready to leave this place and go wherever adventure will take us. Consider this journal entry one, in hopes that if we fail we will live on in the pages of this book.

Perplexed, Banju closed the book. "So my father was an adventurer?"

There was a knock on the door, and Banju hastily ran up the stairs, pushed the lever back down and answered it. A tall muscular man with dark skin was waiting outside the door. "My name is Kossier," the man said in a deep voice. "You must be Banju."

Banju stepped aside and let Kossier in. "Nice to meet you, Kossier." He gestured for the man to sit down. "I don't know how long I'll be gone; it could be months or years before I come back to Smith Village."

Kossier nodded. "I understand. Believe me; I will not disgrace your father's name. The Arrow's Hammer will still be in business when you return, and the house will still be in one piece." He glanced around at the shattered room. "Er...more than it is now, I hope."

Banju picked up his satchel and placed the journal inside it. "Thank you, Kossier, I have no doubt it will be."

Kossier bowed his head. "It is the least I can do for all the things your father did for me over the years."

Banju shook Kossier's hand and gave him a pouch of coins from his belt. "This should help keep things going for awhile. Don't worry if you spend it all; I'm sure there will be a way to regain any losses." His mind flashed to the treasure chest. "Thanks again." With that, Banju walked out of his home to make the final preparations for the journey to Aldor.

The following day, Banju waited by the southern gate of Smith Village for Terin. To pass the time, Banju observed as hundreds of people walked in and out of the village on business. Some who passed gave him strange looks, and he overheard some of them saying:

"Did you hear Thanju's son is going to the tryouts?"

"He is? Oh, dear, he won't last a day!"

"Aldor's no place for a boy of his age!"

"I take it you're leaving without saying goodbye?" someone asked from beside him.

Briefly startled, Banju saw that it was only Gurath. "Uh, yes, Gurath, I guess I was."

Gurath offered his hand, and Banju shook it. "Good luck on your journey, Banju; I hope you accomplish everything you're setting out to do. I assure you that I will not stop praying for you until you return."

Banju smiled politely. "Thank you, Gurath."

As Gurath left, Banju noticed something out of place near the center of town. He waited a few more moments to see if Terin would arrive then went to investigate. There, near town hall, was a small statue of his father surrounded by lit candles and gifts from people in the village honoring his memory. Letters were written displaying their gratitude for the several things Thanju had done for them. Swords leaned off of large crates full of Thanju's favorite foods; Banju saw that even Gurst had set aside one of his prized kegs for this shrine.

The number of gifts shocked Banju; he had been unaware that his father had touched so many people in the last eighteen years. For the short duration that he stood there, he was filled with a small inkling of peace.

"Great, isn't it?" Terin asked behind him.

"Terin! You're late!"

"And you're early, as usual," Terin stated.

"So what took you so long this time?"

"I had to pick up a few last minute items." He whistled, and a donkey appeared with a small rowboat tied to its back. "We won't need our horses."

"Why not?" Banju inquired, a little annoyed.

"I have devised a way for us to reach Aldor twice as fast," Terin said confidently. "If we walk to Elf Lake, we can get into this rowboat and row to the other side, which is only a few hours away from Aldor."

"What about the donkey?"

Terin patted the donkey on its neck. "Ol' Flour here was about to be put down when I found him. He only has a few weeks left before he dies of sickness. We have him carry the boat to the shore for us and then let him roam around free for the last few days of his life."

Banju shrugged. "Okay, we'll do it, but he gets to carry my things until we get there."

They exited Smith Village and treaded down the eastern path. The sun hid behind a blanket of gray clouds and the cool air lightly whirled around them. Dried leaves crunched under their boots.

Despite the autumn conditions, life in the surrounding forest thrived. Fat squirrels sat precariously on fruit trees to gather the last of their winter provisions. In a clearing, geese rested before flying south. Woodpeckers desperately pecked at trees before winter would make it more difficult to find food. Birds of all kinds cheerfully chirped and whistled in the trees, seemingly oblivious to the dreary weather around them.

Banju tried to imagine what the forest must have been like during the time of magic. Through his mind's eye he saw elves laughing and weaving in and out of the trees. The trees themselves were swaying of their own accord and singing in a language that only they understood. A beautiful golden dragon flew by overhead. Banju crossed the bridge connecting the Smithian province to Shallor, and his fantasies vanished.

Terin and Banju spent the night at a kindly farmer's home and continued on their way the following morn. As dusk was settling in the next day, all they could see were the woods that would lead them to the lake. As they entered, they came upon a small stream where Terin suggested they take a break.

The air was brisk and the water from the stream was as cold as ice. The donkey rested on a floor of dry leaves as Terin said, "I don't know about you, Banju, but I think we should keep on going all through the night. The tryouts begin soon, and if we rest for too long, we won't make it in time."

"I agree," Banju admitted, "but there is one major problem: bandits."

"We're both skilled with the sword, Banju," Terin insisted. "If we come upon any bandits, it will be *them* that pay, not *us*."

"Alright, then we'll do it."

Having received his fill of cold water from the stream, Banju stood to leave, but stopped when he saw a doe looking at him from the other side. It was not looking at him with that dumbfounded look that deer often have, but—his breath caught when he realized it—with intelligence. After staring at him for a few moments more, the doe shook its head vigorously. At first he thought that a fly or a mosquito was assailing it, but the way it was quickly and precisely shaking its head from side to side disproved this theory. It was as if it were saying, *"No, don't continue on; turn back. Turn back!"* The doe backed away, then turned tail and ran into the darkness.

"Did you see that?" Banju asked Terin.

"See what?"

"That…that doe over there…"

"I don't see a doe."

"Well, it's gone now, but it—" He stopped, knowing that he would sound crazy if he continued. "Never mind; I must have been seeing things."

"Just keep it together a little longer, will you? I'd like to make it to Aldor in one piece."

They began walking again, Banju on one side of the donkey, Terin on the other, both of them with a hand on their sword hilts. Banju *almost* believed that they would make it through the night without further incident, but that changed a short time after midnight when the moon was suddenly covered by dark clouds.

Banju heard a distant twig snap and saw several dark figures lurking in the tall shadows of the trees. "Terin," he whispered, "there are men following us."

"Are you ready to fight?" Terin muttered, his lips barely moving.

I'd rather not, Banju thought. "Yes."

The bandits stayed in the shadows, matching Banju and Terin's pace step for step.

A spiral of red energy erupted from behind a nearby tree and knocked Banju to the ground. *They have a magician!* he thought with dread and awe. He pushed himself back to his feet as a score of dark clothed men wearing simple masks over their eyes suddenly moved out of the shadows, swords drawn, and charged.

Banju unsheathed Crikkon in time to parry an attack. The bandit twirled his sword skillfully and tried to strike Banju in a sideways combo. When this did not work, the bandit remarked, "Where'd you learn to fight like this, kid?"

Banju blocked another blow, inadvertently cutting off the man's right index finger, and kicked him to the ground. "My father taught me," he replied.

He fought bandit after bandit, knocking some out, wounding others, but never killing anyone. When only a few bandits remained, he thought for sure that they would come out victorious. Unfortunately, more bandits appeared out of the darkness, and they double-teamed him and Terin.

They brutally pushed Banju and Terin to the ground and began to bind them when Terin shouted, "Wait! Stop!"

The man with the severed finger picked up Crikkon admiringly then turned to Terin in distaste. "What do you want, boy?"

Banju was devising a way that he could get Crikkon back when Terin replied, "I have a proposition for you."

One of the bandits stepped out of the crowd and paced toward the leader, twirling red energy in his left hand. "These aren't worth our time. Just kill the one and leave the other to me."

"You know we can't do that," the newly dismembered leader whispered. "We have strict orders that must be followed." He turned his attention back to Terin. "Stop stalling; speak up!"

"Take me as your slave, but leave my friend alone. If he goes free, I promise I won't run, and I'll do whatever you ask of me."

Banju shook his head, quietly untying the loose bindings around his arms. "Don't do this, Terin. We can find another way."

Terin looked at Banju in sorrow and regret. "There is no other way."

The wounded leader thought for a moment, then went over to Banju and lifted him up roughly by the arm. "Very well, boy, I'll hold you to your word." He turned to the other bandits. "Take this 'hero' back to our camp. Five of you, stay here with me while we help this...boy get back on his way."

Banju began to think quickly. They were taking Terin, there was a river leading into the lake a few meters away, the boat was still by him and the bandit had Crikkon in his left hand. *They're not going to let me just walk away.*

Terin was out of sight now. Banju watched in horror as the silhouette of a bandit raised its bow and fired at Terin. A scream ripped through the night air, startling all of the bandits nearby.

When the leader of the brigands turned his attention toward the scream, Banju wrenched Crikkon out of his hand, hit him in the chin with the hilt, grabbed the boat and ran toward the river.

Behind him, he heard someone shout, "After him!"

Banju found himself walking into the strong river, saw his pursuers on both sides of the bank and jumped into the boat. The bandits did not give up and began to throw stones and sticks at him. At one point, the red energy returned and barely missed the boat, instead evaporating a portion of the water behind it.

When they stopped chasing him, Banju began to laugh victoriously—until he heard a deep rumble in front of him. He looked and saw that he would soon be going over a huge waterfall. "Oh, great!" he exclaimed.

Banju was barely conscious when the boat smashed into the water. Despite this, he managed to pull himself back into the boat and lay his head on his satchel. His mind was reeling, and he could just barely make out the trees above him. As the boat continued its autonomous journey down the river, he fell in and out of consciousness. There was one moment where the boat seemed to be pushed by someone else, but he was still too shocked from the impact to be able to see who—or what—it was.

He seemed to be in this mind state for an eternity until he finally came to and sat up. All around him there was dark water and mist. Because of this, he knew he most likely was not on the river anymore and was afloat on Elf Lake. A triumphant laugh wanted to leave his lungs, but he found that something was constricting it within his chest.

When the mist cleared enough, he looked over to the shore and saw a dark rider sitting atop a black horse. The horse was standing close to the water, and the rider seemed to be staring directly at him.

Banju felt an unexplainable sensation; not of fear, but as if something was inside his head, learning his every secret and thought. As this uncomfortable sensation began to ebb away, he decided that he was going to call out to the rider, but then the mist retook the beach. When it cleared, the rider and his horse were gone.

Was I imagining him? He took a deep breath and began to row to the side of the shore that would lead him to Aldor.

○ ○ ○

Adventure Awaits

"Watch your step!" a merchant called to Rik right before he would have stepped on a broken grate and into the water below.

"Thanks," Rik called back as he gingerly sidestepped it and continued on his way. He was job searching again; he had been doing so ever since he had arrived at Dunar three days prior. The coins his father had given him kept Rik from living on the streets, but that could only last for so long in a city like Dunar.

When he had first arrived, he was amazed to find that the rumors about the city "floating" were true. Meaning, it was nearly all at least fifty feet above the ground and the surface of the water. A rocky island supported Dunar's center while the rest of the city had to rely on tall rocks or thick wooden beams to keep it in place. Once one entered the city, it would be nigh impossible to judge that it was different from any other. Its streets were still paved out of cobblestone and granite; tall buildings and thousands of people were all common sight.

But for Rik, that is where Dunar lost its magnificence. Many of the buildings were a boring shade of gray or brown and were in states of disrepair. Being so close to the ocean, the air was always filled with a salty, moist scent. Unfortunately, also being the fishing capital of the kingdom, the air was additionally filled with the stench of dead fish. He was grateful that it was fall, for the smell was likely worse during the hot days of summer.

Through his job searching the last couple of days, he had found that many jobs for fishing, making fishing nets, making fishing poles, skinning fish, sailing fishing boats and cooking fish were available. He sighed and kicked a stone into a grate and down to Dunar's "natural sewage system." Rik scrunched his nose as he imagined gallons upon gallons of waste being dropped into the sea.

He continued his walk, unsure where to go next. If only there was a job where he could utilize the skills that his father had taught him. *Wait a minute.* He stopped and glanced up at Watchtower, the tallest tower located at the city's center. *There is one place.* Hopes renewed, Rik followed the road up to Watchtower. Made entirely of onyx and over ten stories high, the tower stood out like a sore thumb.

Upon asking a guard for directions, Rik was led inside the tower and up a spiral staircase to the office of Paert, Lord of Dunar. His face was wrinkled with age and his bald head was balanced by his black beard; he wore a black tunic with an emblem of the sun rising over the sea pinned to his left shoulder— the crest of the Horizon Guard. The lord looked at him with disinterest. "What do you want, boy?"

"I wish to join the Horizon Guard, sir."

Paert stroked his beard. "How old are you?"

"Seventeen."

"Do you know how to hunt and track?"

"Since I was a child, sir."

"Good. Our numbers have drastically diminished whence His Grace the king announced the knight tryouts. However, I cannot allow just anyone to join without first being tested. Captain Bree is leaving with a hunting squad tomorrow. If you truly wish to join us, you will accompany him."

Rik bowed his head. "Thank you, sir; it would be an honor."

Paert picked up his quill and began to write on a parchment. "Very well. You will find the captain in the stables. I suggest that you check in with him now."

Sure enough, Rik found Captain Bree outside of the stables, a pack slung over his shoulder. Despite his gray beard and hair, Bree was tall and appeared to have the physique of a young man.

"Captain Bree," Rik began.

"What is it?" Bree asked impatiently as he entered the stables.

Unperturbed, Rik continued, "Lord Paert said that I am to accompany you on the hunt."

"A new recruit, eh?" Bree approached a large black horse and began to tie his pack to its saddle. "Then you are prepared to leave today?"

"Today, sir?"

"Aye. The longer we hold off the hunt, the colder our prey's trail will become."

"And what is our prey?"

"Better to tell you along the way." Bree gestured to a gray horse. "You're lucky Bertha there is saddled and ready to go." He mounted his own horse. "Come, we must meet with the other members of our party."

"Now, sir? My horse and all of my belongings are elsewhere."

"Bertha has everything that you need. Now let us be on our way."

Reluctantly, Rik mounted Bertha and followed the captain through the city and out across Dunar's northern bridge.

"What's your name, boy?" Bree inquired.

"Rik, sir."

"Are you new to Dunar?"

Rik fidgeted in his saddle. "Yes, sir. I arrived from Smith Village three days ago."

"Then I'm sure that there is a question on your mind, one that all newcomers have."

"And what is that, sir?"

The captain smiled. "You don't have to end each sentence with 'sir,' Rik; I may be a captain, but too much of our lives are wasted on pleasantries. Now as to the question: I am sure that you are wondering how Watchtower can possibly be made entirely of onyx."

"It had crossed my mind, si—I mean …captain."

Bree laughed lightly. "The south had its elves, but the north had its Cap'Thorians."

"Cap'Thorians?"

"Aye, a race that is lesser known, but their skills in engineering and forgery rivaled that of the elves and the dwarves. It was the Cap'Thorians that built Watchtower and the foundations of Dunar."

Rik glanced behind them at the city's sophisticated design. "What happened to them?"

"The same thing that happened to all other magical races, I suppose," Bree said with a sigh. "They vanished…Though interestingly, it is believed that they disappeared before the Eradication."

They descended into a bout of silence and soon came upon a small camp where three men sat waiting on horseback.

"Well it's about time, captain!" one of them exclaimed. He was a broad-shouldered man at least a couple of years older than Rik with silver eyes, short black hair and a trimmed beard on a strong jaw.

"I was held up," Bree replied. "Ross, this is Rik, a young man wishing to prove himself worthy of the Horizon Guard."

Ross nodded his head in greeting. "A pleasure to meet you. This is my brother Knip," he bore the same face as Ross, but his hair was auburn and his eyes were a mischievous light brown, "and this is Brack." He was a tall, huge man with matted brown hair and a unique spear-axe-sword hybrid strapped to his back. Brack did not acknowledge Rik; he only stared at him with dark, calculating golden eyes. "Oh, don't worry about him," Knip explained. "Brack's a mute; may seem like the silent, mean type, but he's really a jolly and gentle soul once you get to know him."

Brack's eyes narrowed in reply.

Captain Bree swung off of his horse and landed with a bone-crunching thud. "Now that you boys have all been introduced, let's break camp and travel a few miles up the road."

Ross immediately began to strike their tent. "To where, sir?"

"Crown Rock."

They were soon on their way, but not at the pace that Rik had expected—their horses barely moved faster than a walk. However, he did not dare question Bree's technique. The sun was sinking behind desolate hills when they reached Crown Rock, an outcropping of jagged boulders justly named for their circular orientation and sharp ends that pointed to the heavens. Camp was made in its center and a small dinner of salted goat legs was served.

"Rik," Captain Bree said after the meal, "you will take first watch tonight. I know that we are only a few miles from Dunar, but these hills are filled with men just as treacherous as they are. Wake Knip in four hours' time to relieve you. We leave at first light."

Reluctantly, Rik grabbed a thick cloak from Bertha's saddlebags, climbed to the top of one of the boulders and sat staring at the dark and dreary fields and hills that went on as far as the eye could see. The night grew bitter, and Rik wrapped the cloak more firmly around his neck. As he lazily stared up at the stars, the hours began to blend together. There was a sound behind him, and Knip soon scaled the boulder and plopped down beside Rik.

"Sorry; didn't mean to startle you," Knip said. "It's nearly time for my shift, so I thought that I would relieve you a little early."

"Thanks." Rik scooted his way closer to the edge, but thought better of it and asked, "Do you know what we're hunting?"

Knip shrugged. "None of us know but Bree, and he's not tellin'. I'm sure we'll find out tomorrow when we reunite with the others."

"Others?"

"Warren and Cled—trackers who also specialize in gathering information."

Rik began to descend. "Well, I suppose that I will see you in the morning."

"Rik," Knip called out.

"Yeah?"

"I know you're nervous—"

"I'm not."

Knip gave him a knowing look. "You are, whether you want to admit it or not. I want to let you know that you are not alone. In all of our years as Horizon Guards, my brother and I have only been a couple miles outside of the city. This is our first tracking mission, too."

○○○

The Trial of Strength

The wondrous white wall protecting Aldor was over three hundred meters tall and five miles wide. It must have taken several years to complete. Banju stood exhausted outside its twenty-foot high, ten-foot wide entrance. Forcing himself to move, he walked inside; the city was full of tall white buildings made of limestone, and there were thousands of people walking from one building to another. The cobblestone street Banju was on led two miles straight to the huge, glorious marble palace built upon a small mountain. He started walking down the street, stopping at the first inn he came across; the tryouts were not until the following day, and he would need to be refreshed if he was to do well.

After a fitful night's sleep filled with dreams of Terin being taken and slaughtered, Banju headed for the palace, thinking logically that the tryouts would be held nearby.

En route, Banju continued looking around, soaking in the sights and sounds. He had never been in a huge city before; in fact, he had never visited anything out of Smith Village besides brief visits to Bootskin. This city seemed more alive than Smith Village could ever be: the multitudes peopling the streets in their nice, clean, crisp clothing made Banju feel under-dressed in his dirty, torn clothes.

He was nearly to the palace when he noticed that the gate was locked, as well as monitored by ten guards. He sighed and searched for another place that the tryouts could be when he noticed a long line of men waiting to go inside a large domed structure.

Banju walked over to the line and confirmed with the man in front of him that this was in fact where the tryouts were being held. As the line slowly progressed through the entrance, Banju heard a commotion further up the road. He looked and saw a man two hundred meters away sprinting toward him. The man was tall—slightly taller than Banju—and looked to be about the same age. He had golden hair that cascaded down nearly to his shoulders, cerulean eyes and seemed to be in excellent shape. He wore a gray cloak, and a sword in a sheath was tied to his left hip.

"Excuse me, is this where the knight tryouts are being held?" the man asked Banju, gasping for breath.

Banju nodded.

"Great! I know this is an odd request, but would I be able to borrow your cloak for an instant?"

After a moment's hesitation to gather his thoughts, Banju removed his cloak and gave it to him.

"Thanks!" The man put the cloak around his shoulders and raised the hood to cover his golden hair. "Just two other quick favors: May I go in front of you, and if a woman named Shareen comes asking for a man named Stonner, please tell her that you don't know where he is…or something along those lines."

Banju reluctantly switched places with the man, curious as to what this was all about. However, he did not have to wait long, for a flustered red-haired woman soon came stomping to the line. She was young and attractive, with a fire in her eyes and a look of firm determination on her face. One of the shoulders of her red dress was dangling on her elbow, and her hair was frayed.

"Pardon me, sir," she said to Banju, "but have you seen a golden-haired man run by recently? Goes by the name of Stonner."

Banju tried to avoid looking at the cloaked man in front of him. "I'm afraid I haven't."

"Humph." She placed her hands on her hips. "Well if you see him, could you please tell him that Shareen is looking for him?" He nodded, and the woman continued her search down the road.

As she turned a corner, the man gave the cloak back to Banju. "Thank you, my good fellow; I have been trying to escape her clutches for days now." He offered his hand. "The name's Stonner, though you probably already figured that."

"I'm Banju."

"Banju, it is a pleasure and an honor to meet you. So what brings you to the tryouts on this adventure-filled day?"

"Well, being a knight has always been a dream of mine, and this offer gave me the inspiration to travel all the way here from Smith Village," Banju answered, leaving out the fact that his father being murdered was the impetus for his recent decision. "How about you?"

Stonner turned to see how the line was doing, moved forward a few steps and then replied, "My life at Bootskin wasn't going anywhere, so I thought since I'm good with a sword I would do something important with my life; perhaps even make a difference in the world. Though most recently I realized that it was the only way Shareen wouldn't be able to find me."

Banju chuckled lightly, still not recovered enough to fully laugh. *This could be the beginning of a beautiful friendship*, he thought warmly. "Then from this point on, let us make a difference together. And avoid Shareens at all costs."

Stonner grinned and nodded. "Sounds good to me."

The next instant, they were inside the dome and registered. Banju was shocked at the immensity of the obstacles in the arena. There was a large wooden obstacle course with ropes, ladders, platforms and the like that reached up to the top of the dome which was well over fifteen stories high. On the ground, there were a few sparring circles, a large pond and a gravel track that encircled the interior of the arena. Several balconies were strewn at different heights around the training ground's wall, most likely to be used as observation decks.

Banju tried to count the amount of people in the dome but failed each time. He guessed that there were well over a thousand men present. He did not get much more time to think then that, for trumpets blared and everyone who had been speaking grew respectively silent. A muscular young man with long orange hair and the signs of a coming beard walked majestically onto a rostrum near Banju.

When people began to murmur, he raised his hands for silence and they once again complied. "My name is Vince, the son of King Banton. I am here to train you all in the arts of swordplay, archery, jousting, horse riding and a myriad of other skills you will need to become the best knights in the history of Shallor." He paused. "Because of this, you will be facing the Five Trials that men once had to complete to reach knighthood: the Trials of Strength, the Sword, Tactics, Fear and Confusion. There are seven thousand men here today, but not all of you will become knights. By the end of these tryouts, nigh on two thousand will remain. Survival of the smartest and fittest, gentlemen.

"Now, to start things off, the person beside you will be your partner for the rest of the tryouts. That is, if you both make it. I want the first one hundred men closest to me to line up outside of the entrance to the obstacle course."

Banju and Stonner, partners now, were two of the first one hundred to line up. For each pair, Vince would say "defense" and point to the course or "offense" and point to a different entrance to the obstacle course. Banju and Stonner were chosen for offense; they placed all items they would not need on racks and anxiously awaited their instructions.

Vince returned to the rostrum and said, "The people I choose for defense will go to certain spots inside the obstacle course and try their best to stop people on offense from getting through the course." He gestured to a large pile of six-foot-long wooden poles. "Both offensive and defensive teams will use these as a means to defend themselves or fight their way through.

"The ways you are eliminated from this course are simple: you either fall off the course or are rendered unconscious from a defensive or offensive man. If you are eliminated, your path to knighthood will end and you must return to your hometown immediately. But for those of you that pass, you will be ever closer to knighthood." He nodded to the men in the offensive group. "Wait for the defensive men to get in place, then one pair of men can go into the course at a time."

Within the next few minutes the first team went into the obstacle course only to be seen being pushed off a platform into a net below. More teams went in, but none of them made it through the entire course. It soon came time for Banju and Stonner to try.

They climbed the rope ladder to the first platform and walked up a flight of stairs to the second. Two defensive men rushed upon them, but Banju and Stonner deftly defeated them and pushed them off the platform. When they reached the third platform, there was a rocking wooden bridge with swinging wooden pendulums going back and forth across different sections of the bridge. Banju and Stonner gingerly made it to the other side and continued.

After going through more platforms full of defensive men, Banju and Stonner evaluated another difficulty: there was a huge gap between two platforms, two ropes to swing to the other side and two defensive men waiting for them to swing across.

"Time for us to take a more unique approach," Stonner commented as he jumped onto one of the ropes. He swung sideways, holding on with one hand as he grasped the wooden pole with the other. When momentum brought him toward the men, he hit one with his feet, sending that man into the other which plunged them both off the platform. Stonner waved one hand toward the entrance to the next platform and bowed majestically. Banju smiled and swung over. They were almost to the top of the obstacle course now and oddly did not run into any more defensive men. It was when they reached the second to last platform that they discovered why. The remainder of the defensive men—thirty in all—were standing in rows, barring Banju and Stonner's only way off of the obstacle course.

Stonner twirled his pole. "Only thirty? I would have expected more! Let's send `em home!"

Banju spun his pole and placed it in an offensive position. "Yes, let's!"

They attacked with a blinding speed that none of the defenders could match. Many of the defenders would never forget the force of the blows, the broken bones they received or the feeling of falling off the platform and heavily bouncing up on the nets below. What many of them would remember the most, however, was how the attackers seemed to move in unison. Within minutes all of the defenders were either pushed off or lying senseless on the landings.

Banju breathed a deep sigh of relief when the brawl was over. "I don't know about you, Stonner," he bent down slightly, put his hands on his knees and took deep, gratifying breaths, "but there seemed to be a lot more than thirty men."

Just regaining his breath, Stonner replied, "I agree with you all the way." He began to stagger to the long zip line that would take them down to the finish line. "Come on; let's go show everyone that we made it through the first round."

Banju straightened, wincing as he realized how sore his back, legs and arms were. "Alright, let's go." However, before they reached the staircase that would take them to the zip line, there was a grunt behind them. "Wait. There's someone still here."

Stonner sighed. "Come on, Banju, he's not our problem anymore. We made it."

Ignoring him, Banju walked to the side of the platform and glanced over it. There, holding onto a beam for dear life, was a member of the defensive team. He seemed to be younger than Banju, had short black hair and the look in his brown eyes affirmed that he was not going to be letting go anytime soon. "Need help?"

"I must not let go. I must not let go. I must not let go," was his only reply.

"Why are you still holding on? You were disqualified once you fell off."

"I must not—No!" The younger man seemed appalled. "No! The rules clearly state that one is only eliminated if he falls off the platform and into the nets. Technically, I'm still holding onto the platform." He grimaced as his grip on the bar lessened. His voice had a tinge of urgency in it now, "If I let go, I will never become a knight! I can't let that happen! I...must...not... let...go!"

Banju offered his hand. "There is no need for you to hang there all day. Take my hand, and I will help you back up."

The man eyed him suspiciously for a moment, and then seeing that he had no other choice, seized his hand and was pulled back onto the platform. "Th-thank you; no one's ever shown me kindness like that before. What is your name?"

"Banju. And yours?"

"Vren."

Banju shook his hand. "Well, it was nice to meet you, Vren, but my friend and I have an obstacle course to finish. Perhaps we'll see each other again in the later challenges."

"G-good bye, Banju. Thanks again!"

Banju nodded, and then he and Stonner flew down the zip line into the cold pond below. When they slowly staggered onto dry land, they were met with thunderous applause; to Banju's surprise, even the prince was clapping.

Vince shouted, "Come, you two, on the stage with me." When they stepped onto the stage, the prince glared at the crowd and the applause abruptly stopped. He turned his attention back to Banju and Stonner. "Congratulations, gentlemen, you are the first to pass the entire course. A servant will now take you to your quarters where you two can rest for the day. Both of you will be expected back here at dawn. Bring your swords." He shook their hands, smiled and lowered his voice so only they could hear. "I see a bright future in knighthood for you two. Have a good day, and I'll see you both tomorrow."

They bowed their heads and said, "Thank you, sir."

Vince briefly bowed his head in acknowledgment and then turned his notice back to the thousands of men still waiting to tryout. "Now I would like another one hundred to get in line," he said as they walked out of the arena.

Just as Vince had said, a servant was waiting for them. He bowed. "Good afternoon, gentlemen. My name is Matthew, and I will be showing you to your quarters. I also have your things." He handed them the items they had put on the racks and turned. "Please, follow me."

As they did so, Banju began to take in the sites of the huge city again. Each of the buildings he estimated to be over ten stories high: finding a building smaller than that was nearly impossible. It was also almost impossible to find a person not dressed   royally.

Stonner, on the other hand, did not seem impressed by the magnificent city. Instead, he initiated a conversation with the servant. "So, Matthew, how long have you been a servant for the royal family?"

"Almost a decade, sir," Matthew replied in a courteous tone.

"A decade's a long time," Stonner noted, now walking beside the servant. "I'm sure you probably know this city pretty well, then?"

Banju could barely suppress the smile that came to his lips when he realized what Stonner was doing.

Matthew grinned and raised his hands halfway. "Like the back of my own hands, sir."

Stonner smiled with the man and nodded knowingly. "So do you think one of these days you could give me and my friend a personal tour of the city's ins and outs?"

The servant thought for a moment, then said, "Why yes, I think I could do that."

"Thanks, Matthew, that would be wonderful!" Stonner stepped back into pace with Banju.

"Remind me never to cross you," Banju whispered to Stonner.

"I'll take that as a thank you," Stonner whispered back.

They soon walked up to a large, circular building. Matthew opened the door and led them inside. The door was the entryway to a large column of stairs, of which they climbed to what Banju thought to be the fifth floor, and then Matthew opened another door and took them down a corridor filled with even more doors that led to separate rooms. Matthew stopped at one of the doors and opened it. He handed Banju and Stonner a key to the room and said, "This is your room; I hope it is comfortable enough for the two of you."

"Thanks, Matthew," Stonner said, "and we'll see you later about the tour."

The servant smiled. "Yes, sir, we will." He bowed. "Good luck at the tryouts."

"Thank you," Banju and Stonner said simultaneously.

With that, the servant bowed his head and left them so that they could enter their chamber.

The main chamber was circular and had two single beds three feet away from each other, a large wooden dresser, a pantry built into one section of the wall, a small round table with chairs by it, one big shelf that went halfway around the chamber and two lounge chairs with a small table in between them. A door led into another chamber: most likely the refreshing room. On the other side of the first chamber, there was a window with a great view of the city.

They both chose their beds then put their satchels and equipment close by. After that, they debated who would bathe first. Banju won by flip of coin.

The kingdom must be doing very well for them to have a refreshing room in each chamber, Banju concluded. The place to bathe in the refreshing room was not very big—just big enough for Banju to sit in and rinse off. He wanted to remain in the warm, soothing water for a long time, but remembered that someone else still had to use it.

He got out and dressed in his most comfortable tunic then went back into the other chamber. He sat in one of the lounge chairs and looked out at the sun setting over the city while he waited for Stonner to return from the refreshing room. Exhausted, bruised and sore, it did not take long for Banju to slip into a restful sleep.

A Friend for Life

He was back on one of the platforms during the tryouts, but this time, something was different. Stonner was not with him, and instead of the platforms having nets under them and a dome above them, they were outside in a volcanic environment.

Banju went up a flight of stairs, Crikkon held defensively in front of him. There was a bridge right above a volcano, and on the bridge was a man. Not just any man, but the same man with the scar from Banju's previous dream.

The scarred man waved to Banju and said, "Come, join me on the bridge; I need your help."

Despite his better judgment, Banju stepped onto the bridge and walked toward the man. The man smiled and vanished. Banju continued walking on the bridge, confused, until the bridge started to snap, and he fell into the molten lava below.

Banju awoke, still in the chair, still sore, and now he could add a stiff neck and back to the long list of things aching and bothering him. Aside from the moonlight that reflected off of the limestone buildings, the city was dark.

"You couldn't stay asleep, either, huh?" Banju was startled at first, but then he saw that Stonner was sitting next to him. He looked as if he had been up for a long time.

Banju stretched and then replied, "I guess not. How long was I asleep?"

"It's been at least a couple of hours." He chuckled wearily. "I've been sitting here for the last hour or so unable to fall back asleep."

Since they logically presumed that they would not be going back to sleep, they decided to raid the pantry. They returned to their chairs, two bananas in one hand and a cup of a strange tea Banju had never heard of before in the other.

Banju delicately took a sip of the tea and was pleasantly surprised at how good it tasted. From what he could tell, the tea had a hint of raspberry flavor to it, along with herbs and other flavors he could not identify. *I'm going to have to find out what this tea is called*, he thought. He had a reputation of hating teas, but this was an exception.

Banju was pulled from his thoughts when Stonner asked, "So how long have you wanted to become a knight?"

Banju smiled. "All of my life. You?"

Stonner grimaced for a moment and bobbed his head. "It was sort of a last minute decision, really. I was on my own in Bootskin." He paused, seeming to realize that he had not told Banju his life story. "Well, you see, my father died before I was born, so I was raised by my mother in Bootskin. She tried to teach me how to sew and cook...I became rather skilled at these tasks, but as I grew older, I began to want to do other things: boy things. However, my mother wouldn't allow it. 'I don't want you to get hurt,' she used to say.

"Well, one day she had to go up into the mountains to Pass Town for what I assumed was a business meeting or something." He paused again, this time with a slight look of anguish on his face. "Word reached me two months later that she had been murdered on her return home."

"I'm sorry," Banju said in a comforting tone, knowing how terrible it must have felt when Stonner first received the news that both of his parents were now gone.

Stonner continued on, trying not to show any emotion. "The pain I felt that day was unbearable. I fell into a state of depression for over a year, until someone helped me realize that life was still worth living. A kind man approached me one day; he was called 'Saint' by most everyone in Bootskin. He told me that I still had people around me who loved me and could take care of me. Eventually, Saint convinced me to live with him. He taught me how to use all sorts of weapons such as swords, knives, bows and javelins. I began to take my training very seriously and decided that I would find my mother's killer and avenge her death." He took a drink from his tea and then said, "Saint died two years ago from a strange illness. Since then, I have continued honing my skills. When I saw this opportunity to become a knight, I thought it would be a great way to make a name for myself and to increase my skills even further. Perhaps even find out who killed my mother." He took another sip; Banju sensed that he was done speaking, so he decided in the spirit of the moment that he would share his story with Stonner, too.

"I've been living in Smith Village for as long as I can remember; my father rarely spoke of our life prior," he said. "My mother died when I was very young and my younger brother Rik and I grew into the blacksmith business. My father Thanju had acquired fame by opening a blacksmith shop called the Arrow's Hammer.

"We lived a happy and peaceful life until a stranger recently visited Smith Village. Whoever it was had come to kill my father, and unfortunately, he succeeded. After that, I decided to come to Aldor so that I could train myself for a confrontation with the murderer. I don't know if I'll ever find out who killed him...but I do know that I will not rest until he has been avenged."

After that, they sat in silence, finishing their tea and registering what they had revealed about one another.

The silence was broken when Stonner spoke. "I am sorry for your loss, Banju. I've heard many good things about Arrow's Hammer: that's where Saint had all of his weapons made. Your father was a good blacksmith, and I never had a chance to see the shop. Perhaps when this is all over, you could show me around."

Banju smiled gratefully. "I would like that."

At that moment, the sun was almost up, so they prepared to go back to the arena. They tied their swords to their belts, put their boots on, grabbed a handful of carrots and headed toward the arena. As they entered, Banju noted that it seemed to have half as many people in it compared to the preceding day. They approached the main sparring circle where Vince was pacing; he continued to pace for a few more minutes then stood in the center. "Good morning, gentlemen," he said in a loud voice. "Yesterday, over three thousand men were eliminated in the obstacle course. Today it is dawn, and more than five hundred men failed to arrive on time. They will be returning home immediately." He put his hands behind his back. "Let this be a lesson to all of you."

Vince gripped his sword's hilt as he continued, "Today we will be testing how skilled your swordsmanship is. You will all be facing different level instructors in each sparring field. You will all start at a level one instructor, and then continue until you reach the level twelve instructor. If a level one to six instructor defeats you, you are eliminated and must return home immediately. The rules are simple: Don't kill your opponent or severely wound him. Your goal is to knock your opponent out of the circle, disarm him, knock him into unconsciousness or hit him with a mock fatal wound. Might I also add that after this trial, there will be no more eliminations." Confused murmurs erupted throughout the arena, but they stopped when Vince raised his hand. "However, anyone who fails the next challenges will have the opportunity to join the palace guard or train for a normal position in the royal army." Many of the men, including Banju and Stonner, grimaced. Being a palace guard was one of the most boring and uneventful occupations you could ever have, and being an ordinary soldier was nearly as bad. "Form a line, and we shall begin."

There were two rings for each level of instructor, so the men made two lines at the first circles. Everyone in front of Banju and Stonner made it past the first instructor, and soon Banju and Stonner defeated them as well. They fought through each instructor, and Banju did not find it challenging until the last one. Thrust, block; strike, block; Banju could not break through his opponent's defenses. After several minutes of unsuccessful attacks on Banju's part, the instructor began a volley of his own; his intensity and precision rapidly became too much for Banju, and he received a mock fatal blow to his side. Shocked and winded, Banju stepped out of the circle with a wounded pride.

Only one hundred men were eliminated that day; everyone else made it past the level seven instructors and some made it even higher than that.

Vince dismissed them for the rest of the afternoon and told them to return tomorrow.

"I don't know what happened, Stonner," Banju told him as they began their trek home, "my father trained me in swordplay ever since I learned to walk; I should have been able to defeat that last instructor."

Stonner, who had successfully passed the entire challenge, replied, "We all have days where we do not perform our best. This must have just been one of those times." He suspected the true reason for Banju's loss, but did not voice it. "Come on; I'm sure you will redeem yourself at tomorrow's challenge."

Still sulking when they reached their dorm, Banju decided to randomly sift through more of his father's journal until he found something of interest.

Burdick and I have found the Hidden City. I will not name it here for fear of this journal being seen by unwanted eyes. Since our escape from the island, I have not felt as safe as I do here. The inhabitants are a kindly folk the likes of which I haven't seen in any other realm...Burdick asked them today if they knew where the treasure was, but they refused to become involved. I wasn't surprised...

Is it possible to fall deeply in love with someone you just met? While exploring the magnificent sights of the Hidden City, I came across a woman more beautiful than the stars; the moment her soft green eyes met mine, I knew that I loved her. Burdick told me to forget about her, for we would not be staying in the city much longer and must soon continue our quest. "Love and treasure do not go well together," he told me. Perhaps he's right; perhaps I should stop treasure hunting and settle down with her. Regardless, I am going to meet with her tonight. Elaine is her name...has a greater and lovelier name ever been created?

Comforted and inspired, Banju forgot about his defeat.

The next day the contenders met by a huge stable full of horses and unique leather armor that Banju had never seen before.

"Welcome to the Trial of Tactics, men," Vince said as he rode up on his white horse. "Today will be a test of teamwork and strategy. However, only the men I call from this list will be doing the challenge this afternoon; everyone else must come back after supper to see who goes next. Now, I will call the names of one hundred men that will be broken down into four teams." A servant brought him a scroll and he shouted out the names of one hundred men, two of whom were Banju and Stonner.

Once the other men had left, Vince split the men into four teams; luckily Banju and Stonner were left together. "Now here are your objectives for today:" Vince was given another piece of paper, this time a map, "each team will start in different sections of Aldor and must find the other teams and eliminate them." A man walked out of the stable, a padded arrow and short sword in his hands. "The only way to eliminate the other teams is by hitting them with these 'safe' weapons. If you hit them, a powder will spread across the impact radius of their body. Only one team will come out victorious today; the other three teams will be asked to return home or begin their training for the palace guard. Be aware that if you are eliminated but your team wins the challenge, this does not apply.

"Each of you will be given a horse, this leather armor and your choice of these padded swords and arrows; get these items and go to the locations assigned to you. The team that wins shall meet me back at the gates of the palace. Farewell and good luck, gentlemen."

They were all given their armor, horses and weapons and went their separate ways; Banju's team rode their horses to the front of the huge public library.

"So what's the plan?" one of their teammates asked nervously.

"We should probably assign a team captain," another suggested.

"I agree," Banju said, "but might I suggest that we decide quickly?"

"I say we let Banju and Stonner be co-captains," someone in the back proposed. "They were the first ones to make it through the obstacle course and they went farther than nearly anyone else in the sword challenge. Everyone in agreement say 'aye.'"

"Aye," the team responded in unison.

Stonner went with it as if he had known it was going to happen. "Alright, what we need to do is have a front line full of men with swords and a second line of archers. That way, if we run into any unexpected adversaries, we'll be ready for them."

Banju glanced around them and saw that the buildings here were slightly shorter and closer together than any other buildings that he had seen. "What if we had a group of archers on top of the roofs of the buildings on either side of the street?"

Stonner nodded. "Brilliant idea; I will lead one of the groups on the rooftops and you can lead the men down here."

The street was narrow and had a thin sheet of snow over it: the perfect place for an ambush. Banju gripped an arrow in one hand and a short sword in the other. He took a deep breath to clear his mind so that if an attack came he would be ready.

There was shouting up ahead and when Banju and his teammates turned the corner, they saw a group of men on horseback covered in blue powder. Banju smiled up at the rooftops where Stonner saluted back in acknowledgment. *One team down*, he thought, *two to go*.

The rest of the challenge, in Banju's opinion, was a breeze; in no time at all they had successfully defeated the other two teams, only losing three men in the process. He was filled with excitement: soon, he knew, he would become a knight.

They headed for the palace gate where the prince greeted them. "Congrats on your victory," he said. "Your next challenge, the Trial of Fear, will be the most dangerous one yet, so I have come to give you your only clue: araccia. This challenge will be much different from the others, though I cannot divulge how. In three days' time, you will meet me at the main entrance to the city. Farewell."

A Different Kind of Challenge

"What in the blazes is an araccia?" Stonner asked as they returned to their dorm.

"I haven't the slightest idea," Banju replied, "though it does sound familiar."

They had a small meal of honey bread and cheese before they headed out for the streets again.

There was only one place they could think of that would be able to provide information on this topic: the library. To Banju's awe, its exterior was shaped more like a monument than a public building. Marble steps led up to the huge oak doors, and pillars were artfully placed to hold up the overhanging granite roof. The interior was filled with row after row of fifty-foot high columns of books split into two floors for easier access. How anyone could ever find what he or she was looking for in a library so expansive, Banju was not sure.

"Where do we start?" he asked. The only things he had ever seen close to a library were the five full bookcases that his father had kept in his study.

"I don't know; I've never been in a library before."

Thankfully, a kindly looking woman came up and asked, "Can I help you gentlemen?"

"Uh, yes," Banju began. This must be the librarian. "We are looking for information on an 'araccia.' Do you know where we could start?"

A perplexed look crossed her face. "An araccia? What is that?"

"We do not know," Stonner said, "we were hoping to find out here."

"Ah, well, I suppose you could check the encyclopedias. Follow me, please."

They followed her deep into the heart of the library, up a flight of stairs and to a row of thick, black books. "These should help you find what you're looking for; let me know if you need further assistance." Another lost man called out to the librarian, and she left to assist him.

"Well, there's no better place to start than the beginning," Stonner remarked and climbed a small ladder, searching for the letter 'A.' He found it and almost fell off the ladder due to its thickness and weight. Carefully returning to the floor, he set it down on a nearby table. "All it says is 'Araccias, see *Nightmares of the Past* and *The Tale of a Lost Man.*'"

They split up and converged back at the table twenty minutes later when they had found the books.

"What does yours say, Banju?"

Banju flipped through the yellowed pages of *The Tale of a Lost Man* until he found a chapter called "My Encounter with an Araccia." "'I had been wandering in the forest for ten days with no hint of civilization anywhere…Later that day, while I was sitting under a cluster of trees, I heard a sound above me. I was tempted to look up, but to do so may have meant instant death, so I took out my sword and looked through its reflection. The sight that greeted me confirmed my suspicions and sent shivers down my back and arms: it was an araccia. I continued to watch its reflection as I slowly took out my throwing knife from my boot. My hands were shaking now; I would only get one chance. I put the sword down, as if I were going to retire for the night, then spun around and threw the knife right into its throat. It let out a yelp and fell from the tree. Thinking quickly, I grabbed my sword again, beheaded the beast and ran as quickly as I could through the forest. There was no way of knowing if I had really killed it or not…'"

Stonner nodded. "That's a pretty thorough account."

"What does yours say?"

"'Araccias, fearsome beasts with poison-tipped tails, sharp claws and teeth, and a paralyzing breath and stare. They also have the ability to climb any surface and can shoot webbing from their tails to capture their prey similar to a spider. No one is sure when or where they originated, though the most common theory is that they are a result of Zutor's experiments. The earliest account of them comes from *The Tale of a Lost Man*,'" Stonner raised his eyebrows and gestured at the book in Banju's hands, "'which describes how one unknown traveler defeated an araccia unscathed. It is unclear whether this is a true account, however, for meeting one in the forest alone would spell nearly instant death; many unfortunate wanderers could attest to this, if they had survived.

"'Not only is an araccia armed with many lethal characteristics, but it also has attributes that help keep it alive. Its hide is thicker and tougher than it appears, and most notable of all, it has the ability to heal from nearly any injury...Thankfully, during the Eradication of Magic, araccias were driven to extinction because they were believed to derive their special abilities from magic...'" Stonner closed the book, sending a loud echo through the library.

"So we're looking for a creature that has been extinct for centuries," Banju deduced.

Stonner tapped the book lightly as he pondered it. "Maybe, just maybe, it's not extinct." He got up and headed for the exit.

"What are you saying, Stonner?"

"What if the kingdom wanted people to think that they were extinct, but kept some around for special occasions?"

"That's ridiculous!"

"You have any better ideas?"

Banju kept his mouth shut and followed Stonner through Aldor's bustling streets. Unsure where they were going, he was hoping that Stonner would enlighten him soon. Sure enough, when the sun was setting, they stopped outside of a stable on the southern fringe of the city. This part of the city was unlike any part that they had seen before; the buildings were not as bright and many of them were rundown. A brothel was further down the street, and the evening air was filled with the wails of a cat in heat.

The sign outside the stable was heavily worn, but Banju could just barely decipher that it read "Nactar's Animal Care."

Stonner knocked on the door and was greeted by a huge, burly man with a tangled black beard and hair and arms as thick as Banju's thighs. "Yeah? What do you want?"

"Good evening, good sir," Stonner said, "my friend and I were wondering if you happened to know anything about araccias."

The man's bored expression suddenly turned into one of shock and fright and he quickly searched the street to see if anyone was listening in on their conversation. "Shh! Not out here! Please, come in." They entered the shack and were surprised to find it to be neatly organized and clean. Nactar gestured for them to sit in the chairs near his huge desk. "Now, where did you hear that name? Was it Nestril the Jester?"

"No, we heard it from the prince."

Seeing the confused look on the man's face, Banju explained, "We're participating in the king's knight tryouts, and the prince hinted that our next challenge would have something to do with araccias."

Nactar's face softened. "Ah, yes, the tryouts." He sat in his chair behind the desk and clasped his hands together. "Well then, I guess I can tell you, but you must promise not to tell anyone else, nor can you say that you received this information from me." They nodded, and he sighed. "Alright, well, as you may have surmised by now, it seems ludicrous that your next challenge will include extinct animals. However, that is not the case: araccias are still around today."

"But that is impossible," Banju stated. "They were all killed during the Eradication."

Nactar nodded. "Aye, nearly all of them were, 'cept for the ones near Aldor. You see, even through his madness, King Leron recognized that keeping some araccias around the castle would act as natural defenders if the kingdom were ever attacked. To the south of the city gate, there is a small stretch of forest within a deep valley. A barrier surrounds its rim, supposedly because the area is still contaminated by magic. However, there is no magic there, only araccias."

Banju contemplated this. "So the kingdom has kept it a secret for centuries, as a secret weapon to be used in the direst of circumstances. Why bring them into the public eye now?"

The man smiled. "That is why King Banton is so ingenious. I have ways of maiming animals to the point that they won't be as lethal. He approached me months ago and asked me to maim a certain amount of araccias, while he would have the unaltered ones hidden away. When the araccias I have changed are brought into the public, everyone will think that those are the only ones left around. Only he, his son and I know that the real ones are still in existence."

"So really he's creating a false trail."

"Precisely. May I ask why you two sought me out? You seem to be well-versed on the subject already."

"Assuming that Prince Vince continues to keep secret what is in that forest," Stonner edged forward in his seat, "then how do we defeat an araccia? And in what ways have you maimed them?"

"Given their quick healing abilities, it is very difficult to kill one. The best way to stop one is to stab it here," Nactar pointed under his chin. "This will disrupt their brain patterns, stunning them for a certain amount of time. Otherwise, I would hit and run as fast as you can."

"And what changes have you made to them?" Stonner prodded.

"The poison from their tails has been reduced to a brief stun, their eyes and breath can still paralyze you, their claws have been dulled, and their teeth have been shortened to the point that they won't be able to tear you to shreds."

"How were you able to do this?" Banju asked.

Nactar only smiled. "I have my ways. Is that all? I have other work that I need to do. Good luck on your task, gentlemen."

They left then, slightly better prepared than they were earlier that day. Now that they knew that the araccias were not as "hostile," survival seemed no longer an issue.

There was a commotion on the street below, waking Banju before he intended. *No,* he realized with a start when he looked out the window, *it saved me!*

"Stonner, wake up!" He kicked Stonner's bed as he hastily dressed. "We're going to be late!"

Ten minutes later, they were sprinting through the streets to reach the city gate before the challenge started. Luckily they were not late, but they were near the back of the group nonetheless.

Vince soon arrived on horseback, accompanied by ten serious looking knights. "Good morning to you all." He dismounted. "I hope that you have taken my advice on how to prepare for this challenge; that could mean the difference between success and failure. You have all faced defeat by huge numbers and have practiced swordplay and strategy. Now you must face fear itself. I cannot elaborate any further, so let us begin."

At his last words, the immense gate opened, revealing the green flatlands beyond. "Come, let us run to your trial."

Many thought he was joking at first, but when *he* started to run, everyone followed. Two miles in, it was clear that not everyone was in fit running shape: some had to resort to walking, others complained about their cramps and others more were gasping for breath. After four miles, they stopped by a tall metal fence that looped around a forest.

"I will now call out the individuals who will go first," Vince informed them.

"And I'm sure those two 'heroes' Banju and Stonner will go first, as usual," a man quietly sneered behind Banju, sparking a few chuckles.

Banju spun around and came face to face with a black haired man with cold gray eyes. "Yeah, that's right, I mocked you," the man said, inspiring even more chuckles from his friends.

Turning back around, Banju tried to ignore him. "Who is that?" he asked Stonner.

"That's Velberk," Vren cut in, appearing out of the crowd. "He's the jealous type. We used to be friends back in Cebil, until he showed his true colors. I'd watch out, if I were you; he's been upset ever since you two defeated his older brother in the first trial."

Banju nodded and focused on what Vince was saying.

"—challenge will be unlike any you have faced before. Death is a possibility if you are not careful. By unanimous vote, we have decided that this challenge will test only the individual, meaning that you will not be going in with a partner." Several gasped at this prospect. "However, each of you will be accompanied by a guide who will ensure that you have a better chance of survival in the case that you fail." He unrolled a scroll. "The forest has been split into ten sections. I will now call out the names of the first ten to enter: Karst, Triv, Belian, Lort, Pren, Saet, Norm, Stonner, Krem and Rudst."

Stonner clenched his fists, nodded farewell to Banju and stepped forward. Now Banju would have to wait in suspense, hoping that his friend would come out alive and victorious. He sat down on a nearby stump and waited. For the next few hours, all Banju could hear come out of the foggy forest was the occasional scream or unfamiliar roar, most likely from an araccia. Neither the guide nor the contender exited the same way that they entered, so Banju was unsure whether Stonner had made it or not. *Please make it,* he prayed.

Finally, when the sun was casting a red hue over the forest as it descended over the horizon, Banju's name was called. He gripped Crikkon to reassure himself that it was still there and then moved to the front of the assembly.

A thin man with a tired expression greeted him. "Hello, Banju, my name is Alaster, and I will be your guide into the mysterious beyond." Alaster had a bow slung over one shoulder, a shoulder pad on the other and a dozen throwing knives on his belt. He wore thick, tan clothing from head to foot. "Please, follow me; we're to enter in section four."

As Banju followed him along the fence's perimeter, he asked, "So what exactly are you supposed to do once we get in there?"

"I am to follow you and make sure that you survive in the case that you don't succeed. Didn't the prince already explain this to you?"

"I know that much, but isn't it considered cheating to have a guide with you? Aren't we supposed to do this alone?"

Alaster chuckled. "Don't worry; I won't interfere unless I absolutely must. You may not even notice me once we enter."

Banju highly doubted that, but he kept his mouth shut. Just when they were about to enter, a terrible headache split through Banju's skull, sending him to his knees.

"You alright?" Alaster asked with concern.

As quickly as it had come, the headache vanished. "Yeah, yeah I'm fine. Let's get this over with."

With that, Alaster opened the gate that led into section four.

Araccias

As soon as they entered, Banju noticed a complete difference in the surrounding forest. From outside, it looked like an ordinary green forest; but from inside, a light blue hue emanated from every tree, leaf, blade of grass and the air itself. The temperature also dropped, allowing Banju to see his breath in a blue cloud of particles. Every step he took was absorbed into the ground and did not make a sound, even when he stepped on dry leaves or pine needles. It was as if everything had lost its ability to emit sound. In any other circumstance, this may have been considered a placid forest and a place where a flustered man could put his thoughts back together, but here it represented an evil and untamed place which threatened to swallow you whole the first chance that it could.

He withdrew Crikkon, which also did not make a sound, and continued deeper into the magic-tampered woods. He was half tempted to turn around and speak to Alaster, just to see if speech was also silenced, but decided against it in the case that it would summon the beast to their location.

A small wind blew between the trees, brushed across Banju's face and proceeded on its way. Was it just his imagination, or had it halted for a brief moment when it reached his skin? There was no way to be sure, and he was not sure he even wanted to know.

Suddenly, a purple bird fluttered onto a nearby branch, its feathers accentuated by the blueness of the air. He stopped, anticipating what it was going to do, and was shocked when the bird let out a long, elegant whistle. After not hearing a single sound for so long, the whistle seemed amplified a hundredfold and out of place in this dangerous place. Its song ended, and it looked Banju right in the eyes before taking flight and disappearing into the blue leaves. The sooner this was over, he decided, the better.

They came upon a patch clear of trees, and Banju saw the strangest sight yet. The sky had been morphed into a light violet with twisting, swirling blue and red clouds. Had they passed into another realm when they walked through the gate? Stories of old mentioned gateways that could lead to places such as this. Or had magic been prominent in this forest for so long that the surrounding environment had been transformed into a strange new world?

His headache returned, stronger than ever, but once it subsided he could have sworn that images had flashed behind his closed eyes. This did not surprise him as much as he thought it would, however, for his mind had seen many strange things in here already, so it only seemed logical that the magic in the air was beginning to take effect on him. When he reached that conclusion, he stopped. The deeper he went, the stranger things became; he decided to stop before insanity could take complete control.

Nearby, he could see Alaster heading for a side path previously hidden from view. Banju grabbed his arm. When he gave him an inquiring look, Banju decided to risk speaking. "Don't go that way," an image of Alaster being swallowed by the path crossed his vision, "bad things over there."

Alaster did not respond, instead retracing his steps until Banju could no longer see him. A distant scream permeated the air, and Banju knew that one of his fellow contenders had just found an araccia in section three or five. This inspired him more than anything else to find his prey and end it right here, right now.

Consequently, the hairs on the back of his neck suddenly stood on end and his mind became clouded as if he had just woken from a deep sleep. He backed up against the nearest tree and used Crikkon's reflection to search the surrounding foliage for anything suspicious. For several blood-pumping moments, nothing happened, but once he thought that he had seen movement in the tree to his right.

He closed his eyes to avoid coming into contact with the araccia's paralyzing stare and was soon bombarded by a vision of it attacking Alaster instead. A few seconds later, he heard another scream. However, this scream was closer than the other one; it seemed loud enough to be coming from this section itself. But that was impossible, for only Banju and—

His eyes snapped open and he sprang into action. "Alaster! Alaster, where are you?" There was a small, rumbling, echoing growl further down the path, so he sprinted down it and called Alaster's name several more times at the top of his lungs in the hopes of drawing the creature's attention to him.

The sight that greeted him stopped him in his tracks and threatened to force him to run as far away as he could as fast as he could. Alaster was on the ground, arms covering his head for protection, being clawed and bitten by a blue creature that had the body of a cat-dog, the claws of a lion and a tail that reminded Banju of a scorpion's, only much bigger and furrier. Its head was slightly longer and wider than a dog's and was supplied with short, razor sharp teeth. Thankfully he could not see its eyes; otherwise he would have been unable to do anything to help Alaster.

"Hey, you, over here!" He threw a blue stone at its furry ribs. The araccia grunted, stopped mauling Alaster and turned to face this new annoyance. Banju spun around and looked at it through Crikkon's reflection. It snarled and leapt for him, but he ducked at the last minute and managed to slice the side of its hide open.

When it crumpled to the ground, he ran over to Alaster to see if he was still alive. Aside from a few deep scratches and a slightly torn right arm, he seemed no worse for wear. "Did...did you kill it?"

Banju nodded. "Yes, I think I did."

"Did you stab it beneath its chin?"

"No, I—" He stopped, suddenly remembering what Nactar had told them. "I cut open its hide. Come on, we need to get you out of here before it finds us again. What's the quickest way out of here?"

He helped Alaster to his feet, who nearly fell due to a previously unseen gash in his leg. "Don't be foolish. Take it out while it's down; cut off its head and then you can worry about getting us out of here."

Banju set him down beside a nearby tree trunk and then cautiously went back to the spot where he had fought the araccia. There he found only a blue pool of blood. "Oh great," he murmured, raising his sword and circling the area. The forest fell back into its eerie silence, but this time there was a new level of suspense to it.

At that moment, the headache returned, bringing with it another blur of images. Through his mind's eye, Banju saw the araccia leap from above and pin him to a tree. He instinctively jumped to the side, just missing the real araccia attack his former position and hit a tree.

He ran with all of his might, subconsciously aware that the beast was following him in the treetops. A root sprang out of nowhere, tripping Banju before he had ran more than two hundred meters. As he tumbled silently yet brutally down a forested hill, he lost his grip on Crikkon and was stabbed several times by thorn bushes, rocks and low-hanging branches. Luckily or unluckily, his fall was brought to a stop when his stomach came in contact with a rotting tree trunk.

Winded and bleeding in dozens of places, he laid there waiting for the inevitable. There was an unusual and fearsome growl off to his right. He continued to lie there, hoping the trunk would protect him from the araccia's line of vision. Realizing that this would not be enough in the long run, Banju began to grope around for Crikkon. The growl returned, closer this time. He stopped searching and turned around.

So this is it, he thought. There on the trunk was the araccia. Banju struggled to his feet and shakily ran behind a tree. Just in time, too, for the araccia pounced moments later and followed him back through the forest. He sprinted around in a wide circle, still looking for Crikkon but concerned for his life more than anything else.

Suddenly, the araccia jumped out from the trees to his left and brought him to the ground. He closed his eyes to slits so that he could hardly see then held his arms out to hold the creature at bay. It was strong, stronger than he had thought it was, and would soon break free of his grip and have a clear shot at his throat. As it grew closer, he risked using only one arm so that he could search the surrounding area with his free one for anything that could help him. His fingers closed around a large stone and he brought it up and hit the araccia's head as hard as he could.

The beast went limp, and Banju slowly crawled away from it, still desperately looking for Crikkon. Only seconds passed before he heard the all-too-familiar growl. He sighed and doubled his efforts, now running as fast as his bruised and bleeding legs would take him. His mind's eye saw the araccia pounce upon him from behind, so he jumped to the ground and to the right just before the araccia did precisely as he had seen. It growled in frustration and turned to attack him again.

That is when, to his great relief, he saw Crikkon lodged between a rock and a fallen tree twenty feet behind the monster. If only he could maneuver around the araccia and reach it. *There is only one way to do this.* Banju charged the araccia and leapt at the very last moment, sailing inches above its claws. When he landed, he nearly fell to the ground in pain, but his survival instincts kept him going. He heard it following close on his heels but did not care anymore; if he was going to die, he was going to die fighting.

He jumped the last few feet to the weapon, wrapped his fingers around the hilt and spun to face his pursuer, nicking its chin with the blade. The araccia howled and veered to the right, hitting the fallen tree. Banju was not going to give it another chance; he raised Crikkon above his head and brought it down upon the beast's neck. Greenish-blue blood spouted out of its open neck, sizzling when it came in contact with the tree's bark.

Banju breathed deeply in relief and leaned against the tree. It was finally over. After catching his breath, he fashioned a walking stick and slowly and painfully began to walk back to where he had left Alaster. The guide had not moved a muscle from the trunk where Banju had placed him.

"Did you—Is it dead now?" he asked nervously.

Banju nodded, and a small smile crept to his lips.

Alaster smiled as well, and together they limped with difficulty to a different gate that led them out of the forsaken forest. They stopped before opening it, both realizing that they had feared that they would never see the other side of the gate again. Banju opened it and they walked back into the world of green and natural color.

○○○

The Beast in the Night

On the morrow Rik and the others continued traveling northward. The Smith Mountains could be seen to their left, and the ground grew rugged beneath them. Dark clouds reigned above, and the cold air bit at the unprotected parts of their skin. Captain Bree rode in front, his face expressionless; he still had not shared any information with them.

It was sometime after lunch that they spotted gray buildings in the distance.

"Warren and Cled await us there," Bree presented. "Be careful around the townsfolk; they are jumpier than most."

They arrived at the hamlet, a cluster of stone buildings and grim inhabitants who gave them wary looks as they passed. Two men garbed in brown cloaks awaited them in the village's center.

"Captain Bree," one greeted. His long black hair was braided, and scars disfigured his face.

"Warren," Bree replied. "I trust that you were successful?"

The man beside Warren spat to the side. "Aye, there's something here. We found a farmer who claims to have been attacked. He wants to meet you."

"Very well, Cled; lead the way."

Cled eyed the others suspiciously—Rik grew uncomfortable because the man only had one eye—and then he spun on his heel and led them back outside the village and to a crudely built farm.

A man with dark circles under his eyes rushed up to them. "Thank the Creator! You have come!" His voice quivered with an unknown fear. "Please, follow me to my field."

They dismounted and fell in step with the man. As they went over a hill and into the field, a sickly smell intruded their senses. *Death,* Rik realized.

A cow lay sprawled on the cold ground, its head turned an ashen black and its innards splattered around it. Bree covered his nose with his forearm and crouched near its head. "When did this happen?"

"L-last night," the farmer replied, standing ten feet further away than everyone else. "I heard her scream…" He shuddered. "It is not a sound I wish to hear again. I then went out to see what had happened…I found her like this."

The captain carefully prodded the head with the tip of his dagger. "What did you lose?"

"A few chickens and rabbits…a-and her heart."

"Her heart?" Bree stood and unceremoniously backed away from the corpse.

"This isn't the only farm to be attacked," Warren added. "Other farmers in the area reported hearts missing from some of their animals, as well as the heart of one unfortunate farmhand."

Captain Bree turned and surveyed the field. "We need to search for any tracks leading to the corpse or away from it."

The others complied. "What do you think this is?" Ross asked. "A predator from the mountains?"

"No." The captain spat. "I think it's magic."

"Magic?" Warren asked, his mouth twitching. "This ain't no fairy tale, captain."

"Bree may be on to something." Knip knelt and pointed to something on the ground. "Look at this."

Cled complied. "Coyote tracks?"

"It's something else," Knip insisted. "It's glowing."

Knip was right; the track glimmered with a faint green and red light. Everyone backed away as if it were about to shower them with poison.

"Seven sirens," Cled gasped. "This is not what I thought I would be doing when I joined the Horizon Guard. I'm going back to Dunar; if the rest of you have any sense, you should do the same."

Captain Bree did not say a word until long after Cled's departure. "If anyone else wishes to leave, do so now. No penalty or dishonor will befall you." When no one did, he said, "I cannot guarantee that we will come out of this alive; we are dealing with forces centuries old; but we must stop this threat before it reaches Dunar. Knip, Brack: go into the village and replenish our supplies. Warren, find where these tracks go. We follow them as soon as we are ready."

Within the hour, they were slowly riding to the northwest. The wind whipped at the ends of their cloaks. Rik tried to keep his head clear for the possibility of an attack, but his mind kept returning to the gruesomely mutilated cow. *If magic could do that to that cow, imagine what it could do to us.*

Ross was voicing this very fear, "Captain, after seeing what happened to that cow, do you think it wise for us to continue our hunt? Would it not be wiser to send word to Dunar and return with greater forces?"

Bree shook his head. "Wiser, yes, but by then this killer may disappear or find reinforcements of its own."

"You know where this trail will take us, don't you?" Warren implored.

The captain glanced ahead of them before replying, "I know full well, Warren. If you have grown craven since last we met, then you can still turn around."

Warren did not respond; seizing the opportunity, Rik rode up beside him and asked, "What lies ahead?"

"Woodsbane."

Dread seeped into Rik. "But Woodsbane is on the other side of the mountains."

Warren bobbed his head. "So the stories say. Think about it: the Drifters trapped all monsters and forces of darkness within that forest; little did they know that there was a narrow pass that spills a section of the forest outside of the mountains."

"You actually believe the stories?"

"I have no reason to doubt them." Warren repositioned his reins. "Do you?"

"No." Rik remembered Terin and his disbelieving attitude. *If only he could see where we are about to go.* "Do you think that whatever attacked that village escaped from Woodsbane?"

Warren shrugged. "Anything is possible now. Woodsbane has been tainted by magic for hundreds of years; I'm more concerned about what we might come across in there."

Rik imagined coming face to face with a beast from Gurath's tales and shivered. "Hopefully we can find our prey before that happens."

"Best prepare for the worst," Warren said grimly. "It may be the only difference between life and death."

○ ○ ○

Warrior's Maze

After the challenge, one week of recovery and then two weeks of training and conditioning followed. Out of the several things that Vince made them do, jousting, sprinting and swordplay stood out the most to Banju.

The morning after the brutal two weeks of training, they found a letter outside their door informing them to go to the royal gardens instead of the arena. Banju and Stonner were unsure what to expect; nonetheless, a slight feeling of nervousness encapsulated them both.

When they reached the gardens, a servant led them down a path. Banju was impressed at how short Aldor's winter was; he had only been there for less than two months and already there were barely any signs of snow. In Smith Village, there would still be snow for another two to three months; in Aldor, however, the grass was already returning to its richly green self, the trees were growing buds and the flowers were beginning to blossom. The temperature during the day was usually mild, with a few odd cold days here and there, but the nights were still bitterly cold.

The garden was immense: over two miles in circumference. Part of the garden was a small valley by a large maze made completely out of tall hedges. The other parts of the garden had orchards with all types of fruits and hundreds of rows of flowers.

Banju and Stonner made it to the maze a few seconds before everyone else, giving them the opportunity to stand in the front line close to a large oak tree that Vince was sitting leisurely by. There were just three thousand men left in the tryouts, and this was the last of the Five Trials.

Vince shifted his position on one of the giant roots of the oak tree. "Welcome, gentlemen," he said with a smile, "before I tell you the details of this challenge, I think it is important to tell you the significance of this location." Vince's smile was replaced by a look of great pride and reverence. "Almost six hundred years ago, Marek Warriorborn was followed to this very location by his sworn-enemy, Vaelkrixx, and his huge army. There was no palace or civilization here at the time," he added.

"Marek ran into this maze with the faith that he could defeat the entire army by himself. Using all of his experience, he managed to kill all of Vaelkrixx's men, one by one. In the exact center of the maze Marek fought Vaelkrixx to the death and came out victorious.

"Not long after, he built a palace close to the maze to remember his great victory. Soon this palace became the center of a small kingdom Marek called Aldor." He paused reverently. "Marek's great grandson became the famous leader and warrior that we know as the Great King.

"This challenge, I must say, is the second hardest one you will face—araccias, I would assume, would take first—but it is also your last one." Many men gasped in surprise. "That's right," Vince said, his smile returning, "once this challenge is over, those who make it through will be anointed as knights. I am pleased to say that you have all performed valiantly in the challenges thus far."

Velberk, standing near Banju and Stonner, asked, "What do we need to do?"

Vince glanced down at Velberk and replied, "All of you must enter this maze and come out on the other side. Those of you that can't make it through by sundown will be sent home or to the palace barracks. This is the final, but decisive, elimination." He raised his left index finger. "There is a catch, however: the first few men that make it through will be given the rank of captain among a squadron of knights." He clapped once. "Good luck!"

Banju and Stonner were one of the first men to enter the maze, and Banju was almost overcome by the claustrophobic feeling of the hedges that towered over them—the hedges were so tall that they blocked out nearly all sunlight.

It did not take long for most of the men to go down separate paths, leaving Banju and Stonner alone. Each path was a winding headache, and most of them led to frustrating dead ends. Every once in a while, Banju and Stonner would reach a dead end, and many times they would retrace their steps and try a different path.

It was almost sunset, and no one had made it through yet. Banju felt like he was almost there, going on instinct instead of what he could see in front of him. By luck, he and Stonner discovered the exit to the maze.

Vince was waiting, arms crossed, pleased with their victory. "Congratulations, Banju and Stonner, you have become captains in the royal army." He unsheathed his majestic sword and told them to kneel. "By the power invested in me by my father, King Banton III, ruler of the majestic land of Shallor, I dub thee, Banju," he placed the flat end of his blade on Banju's shoulder and then placed it on Stonner's, "and thee, Stonner, knights of the royal kingdom of Shallor. Rise, Sir Banju, Sir Stonner."

Banju rose, a mixture of happiness, pride, excitement and fulfillment swelling up within him. He was about to convey his gratitude when Vince grabbed his arm and whispered to them both, "There is a covert operation I need carried out. Are you two interested?" After they nodded, he continued, "I'll give you more information tomorrow, but for now return to your quarters and act as if I never asked you to do anything. Congratulations, again." Vince stood up and went to greet the next person to conquer the maze: Velberk. "Congratulations, Velberk, you are now a commander in the royal army."

Velberk looked at Banju and Stonner with jealousy and hatred. He whispered to one of his friends and continued to glare at them.

"I think that we've just made an enemy," Stonner whispered to Banju.

"So do I," Banju whispered back. "Let's just hope that he doesn't try anything stupid."

"Yes, for his sake."

○○○

The Dark King

Strong wind whistled through his castle, as if a chorus of ghosts were howling in unison. The corridors were kept dark and hot, just the way he liked and remembered them. Makir had been changed forever when he first started using the Gauntlet. It was once a hot, dry place, but now Nature had played a cruel trick and turned it into an icy volcanic land. If only he knew then what he knew now.

However, as time went on, he had begun to like this new cold, snowy climate. Severe blizzard conditions made it easier for him to control and raise prices on supplies to the cities and larger villages. Not to mention that it also made it easier for his troops to covertly perform their orders. For this reason, many had come to fear storms.

A guard saluted Sarkk as he walked through the door to his private chambers. Few knew that his "private chambers" was actually a courtyard filled with trees, flowers, a pond and many other beautiful things of nature—all untouched by the pitiless cold. He sat by the pond on a bench he had made. This was the only place where he could find peace, the only place where he could communicate with the Dragon Lord.

He clenched his Gauntlet hand, seemingly bringing the trees together near him. When he realized this, he released his grip. *I must talk to him soon.*

He remembered that day years before when the Dragon Lord had first contacted him. Things had been different then; he had been a farmer with a wife and two children. Certainly, plowing a desolate field may not have appealed to everyone, but he had been happy.

It just so happened that on a day when he was plowing his field that a man materialized out of the dust and began to speak to him. Promises of great power and fertility throughout the land had been given, if Sarkk would only form an alliance with the Dragon Lord. The offer was too tempting for Sarkk to refuse. The dust figure then led him to the grounds in front of his ancestor Narkk's abandoned castle and told him to start digging. Within the hour, Sarkk uncovered the one thing that man simultaneously feared and coveted: the Golden Gauntlet. The Dragon Lord instructed him to place it on his hand. Sarkk knew now that he should have thrown it into the nearby lava river right then and there.

After weeks of learning what the Gauntlet could do, the dust figure left him to do with it as he pleased. *Where to start*, he had thought. He had turned his field into a glorious garden. His wife had been so proud of him; he remembered well the loving words she had spoken to him and the kiss that had followed. His blissfulness was to be short-lived, however, for he soon discovered that the produce he had created was severely poisonous. Never again did he want to see a child bite into a carrot and immediately fall to the ground and writhe in pain while their life ebbed away, or see a woman slowly deteriorate from the inside out as the salad she had eaten ate away at her innards.

Insanity and rage overcame him, leading him to level an entire town with only a mere thought. He did not stop there, however. Using the devastating force of a hurricane, he had brought the population of a city on the coast to zero. Crops and livestock supporting those further inland were incinerated. It was not long before all in Makir knew his deeds. People worshipped him and offered him gifts and sacrifices; this only had infuriated him more, for he had no desire to be a deity.

The dust figure returned, this time explaining to Sarkk that to refuse these offerings was foolish. With his newfound power and fear, he could gather an army and destroy Shallor, which was responsible, he said, for bringing the Gauntlet into existence in the first place. Sarkk had reluctantly agreed and took up his home in Narkk's castle as the all-powerful ruler of Makir.

That was when things had begun to change. The devastation he had caused earlier was responsible for the snow and ice that plagued Makir now. In addition to the manipulation of the land itself, his body was morphed, as well. He grew another foot and a half, gained muscle mass and many of his bones expanded—several, especially in his arms, broke through skin and turned into small spikes. He hardly recognized himself anymore.

Despite what the Dragon Lord had told him about Shallor, the fact remained that it was the dust figure that had introduced him to the Gauntlet. *I really need to speak to him.*

As if in response, the water at the center of the pond began to swirl and rise, slowly making the shape of a man. Once the liquid figure took full shape, it began to walk across the surface toward him. A cloak formed around it, taking on a dark red tint. The figure walked on solid ground and stood in front of him, arms crossed.

Sarkk knelt to the imposing figure. "Dragon Lord," he said with as much respect as he could muster, trying to hide his feelings of resentment.

The figure's face finally formed completely, revealing the ugly scar on the left side of his face and his cool blue eyes. Those eyes bore into him, and he knew that he had failed to hide his feelings. "King Sarkk," the Dragon Lord said in his cool tone. "I like what you've done with the courtyard."

Sarkk nodded halfheartedly in gratitude. "And to what do I owe the honor of your presence?"

The Dragon Lord gestured for him to stand. "I have come to warn you."

Sarkk almost laughed. "*You* came to warn *me*? Why not have one of your spies do it for you?"

"It has been long since last we talked." He seemed not to notice the sarcasm. "I wanted to check in on you and your forces."

"Then what have you come to warn me about?"

"Shallor has gathered its forces." He moved, and a few drops of water fell. "The prince himself has trained an elite group. They are planning to attack you, Sarkk."

"What if they are going to attack you instead?" Sarkk shot back.

"They will not attack Raktin because of the treaty that they made with us two hundred years ago." He chuckled. "The fools think we won't ever attack them. Their time is coming…"

"But you insist that I wait for them to come to me, instead of the other way around?"

"It is all part of my excellent plan. They will attack you, you will either destroy their forces or bring them down considerably and then I will attack with forces of my own. Their land becomes our land, their people our people; Raktin and Makir will be the dominant kingdoms once more."

"No!" Sarkk pounded on the bench, shattering it into splinters. "This is *not* the way that I had it planned. I am tired of your games! What if we lose, hmm? What then? You would rather have me sacrifice my men and my land just so that your 'excellent plan' will come into fruition!"

The Dragon Lord raised his hands, sending many drops flying. "Now, Sarkk, let's not get too carried away."

"You listen to me," Sarkk pointed a finger just inches from the figure's face. "This is how it's going to happen: I'm going to build up my forces, and *I* will attack Shallor. Once I have defeated them, I will destroy you!"

The Dragon Lord's face became stern and his eyes became as dark as the darkest of shadows. "Must I remind you who informed you where the Golden Gauntlet was? Who trained you how to use its power? Who made you the ruler you are today?"

"You ruined my life from the start!" Sarkk roared. "I could have become a peaceful farmer and forgotten my family heritage, but you had other plans! You also knew that the Gauntlet would have negative effects on the land, yet you kept those details a secret from me! Not only have you ruined my life, but the lives of everyone in Makir! I will not let you do it anymore. Your power over us has ended, *Dragon Lord*; I am the only power that matters here now."

The Dragon Lord sighed. "I knew that it would eventually come to this. Realize that if Shallor comes—and I know it is—we will not be there to assist you."

Lightning struck, the wind picked up and Sarkk's voice boomed like thunder. "Get out of my sight, you filthy bastard!" He gestured with his hand, and the water keeping the figure in tact suddenly exploded, hung in the air for a moment and returned back into the pond.

He sighed, and the severe weather suddenly stopped. The beautiful courtyard was now filled with charred remnants of its former splendor. He walked to each remain and touched them with the Gauntlet, restoring them. Sarkk gripped a black plant that he kept wrapped around his left arm at all times—the plant that had killed his wife. Once he calmed, he bolted out of the door.

"Guard, get my generals and have them meet me in the central chamber; we have battle plans to discuss."

○○○

A Long Awaited Tour

Banju and Stonner's restful sleep was cut short by a brief knock on the door. Stonner groaned and rolled over in his bed, but Banju snapped into action, putting on his boots and a clean shirt, fixing his hair and answering the door.

Vince stood outside the door, and once Banju ushered him inside, he said, "Peace may come—"

Banju recognized the old saying and finished, "—but chaos must come first."

Vince smiled. "You know your history."

Banju nodded and gestured for Vince to sit down in one of the lounge chairs. "Yes, it's what King Leron said before the Eradication of Magic began."

Vince looked out the window as if searching for something. "That was perhaps the most memorable and horrifying time period in our history." Vince turned his attention back to Banju. "My father used to quote that line all the time when Aldor had trouble with a band of raiders or the economy spiraled downward." Without looking, he pointed a thumb where Stonner was sleeping. "Wouldn't get up, eh?"

Banju smiled and shook his head. "No, he's exhausted. It's even difficult for him to wake up on a normal day."

Vince leaned in closer and his voice dropped almost to a whisper. "The reason I came here, as I'm sure you've guessed by now, is to give you the briefing for the mission. About a week ago, one of the most dangerous, cunning and notorious criminals escaped from one of our prisons. We have kept the city under lockdown, but soon we fear that that won't be enough to stop him.

"His name is Kyron and your mission is to bring him back into custody or, if necessary, kill him. In three days' time my father will be having a banquet; you and Stonner will be attending as guests of honor. However, the real reason you two are coming is because we fear that Kyron might break in and try to assassinate someone of high rank, steal something of value or something so sinister we can't even comprehend.

"You and Stonner will be there to find and stop him." He paused in thought. "And be aware that Kyron never works alone; he always has a partner. Any questions?"

"I have one." They looked back in surprise and saw that Stonner was now wide-awake. His hair was sticking up in many places, making his head look like the top of a human tree. "What did Kyron do to get all of this attention attracted to him?"

Vince spoke as if he was chewing on poison. "He killed a score of civilians and knights, he stole many rare things from a museum and he attempted to kill Corbin, Lord of Cebil."

"So I'm guessing you probably want him dead instead of just stopped," Stonner predicted.

Vince nodded grimly. "If you two don't do it, he will most likely face a terrible public execution."

"So we have full permission to kill him?"

"And any of his compatriots."

Stonner stroked the small stubble growing on his chin thoughtfully. "Then it will be done, sir."

"Do we know what he looks like?" Banju asked.

"He has one very noticeable feature," Vince made a zigzag pattern across the entire right side of his face with his index finger. "He has a lightning-like tattoo that goes down his face. He may try to cover it with a hood or hair, so be on the alert."

"May I ask why he has such a tattoo?" Stonner asked.

"Ask him when you find him." Vince stood and turned to leave. "I must go before anyone notices that I left. I will be in touch. Remember: don't tell *anyone* about this."

"We won't," Banju and Stonner said in unison.

Once Vince left, Banju said, "So what do you think?"

"I think it's time for some breakfast."

Banju rolled his eyes and they went the rest of the day without discussing Kyron.

The next morning they found a package with a letter on top of it that read,

Banju and Stonner:

Here are some books and some equipment for the event in two days. Read the books and stay alert!

Prince Vince

They soon discovered that the books were manuals on how to act properly at a banquet. Two dress suits, conveniently Banju and Stonner's sizes, were laid out as well. At the bottom of the package there was a small book that had Kyron's entire criminal history in it.

After reading some of the manuals for half the day, Banju said, "Do you think that we should familiarize ourselves with the banquet hall and the surrounding areas?"

Stonner closed the manual he was reading with a dramatic *thud*. "Sounds good to me; and I know exactly who could give us a tour."

Reading his sly grin, Banju caught on. "Matthew?"

"Matthew."

The banquet hall was outside the main gate to the palace but was separated by a street that circled around it. Banju and Stonner knew that they were not allowed into the hall, so they went directly for their main target.

"Do you know where we may find a certain servant by the name of Matthew?" Stonner asked a guard at the palace's gate.

"Last I saw of him, he was headed for the royal gardens," was the reply.

"Thank you kindly."

They found him right where the guard said he would be: sitting on a bench by a row of lilacs.

"Matthew, my good fellow." He nearly jumped at the sound of Stonner's voice. "We did not catch you at a bad time, I hope?"

"No, of course not, sirs," Matthew said with a weary smile. "It is my understanding that congratulations are in order: I heard that the two of you passed the Prince's tests with flying colors."

Stonner shrugged. "Oh, it was nothing, really. Say, do you recall that time you promised to take us on a tour of the city? Banju and I were wondering if you would be willing to take us on one now; we hate to keep people waiting to fulfill their promises."

"Ah, yes, a tour!" Matthew exclaimed. "It is a shame that the Prince has kept you locked away in flurries of combat and wit! No time to explore a city, I presume. I would be honored to take you gentlemen on a tour!" He tapped his chin, clearly transformed and excited by the thought of it. "Where to start, where to start... The Rainbow Fountains are not far from here, the park is only a few blocks from that, and the monuments and museums are of course near there. Which would you like to see first?"

"We were thinking the business district near the palace, specifically," Stonner broke in.

"Why, yes, that would be a good place to start! Many shops around here; not many attractive sights, though."

"That would be great to end with," Banju said.

"Of course! Why didn't I think of that? Smart boys, you both are. Come; let's get started!"

There were many buildings close to the hall, most of them shops and bakeries. A few tall business buildings stood a few stories higher than the hall, and Banju calculated that these buildings would be the ideal place for someone who wanted to sneak into the hall unannounced.

"Here we have several of the most delightful and elegant stores and businesses in the entire city," Matthew explained. "Over there is Ronell's Café and the Underground Saloon. To our right is the Royal Robe and—ah, yes!—the Banquet Hall where only the most important and regal balls and other festivities are held.

"As you may have noticed, there are many tall business buildings surrounding the palace. These were designed to hinder invaders from reaching the palace and to—"

"—act as archery stations for the city's defenses?" Stonner concluded.

"Why, yes, as a matter of fact. It is believed that when this city was being built as Shallor's capital, King Marek wanted it to be heavily fortified in the case that pillagers attacked. Even until the Great King's rule—"

Stonner cut in again, "Do you think that one of the business owners would allow us to go on his roof? It would be quite a memorable experience to see the city from such a height."

"You would have to ask," Matthew seemed unperturbed by Stonner's bluntness. "I will wait here if you would like to go; heights and I do not mix well together."

They entered the building nearest to the hall and were immediately greeted by the courteous owner. When they asked him, he said that he would be delighted to allow them access to his roof. Banju thought this strange, for he had not asked them for an explanation to their actions. *If it was this easy for us,* he reasoned, *Kyron could have just as easily done this as well.*

The roof of the building was flat, allowing Banju and Stonner perfect maneuverability around it. From his new vantage point, Banju could see that this building was close to many of the other tall buildings—close enough together that someone could effortlessly jump from one building to the other. He peered over the edge and saw that there was a clear line of sight into one of the hall's ceiling windows: perfect for someone to snipe or jump through. However, he thought that it would be impossible for someone to jump down onto the banquet hall from this height without serious injury.

They thanked the owner and reunited with Matthew. "Hello! How was it up there?"

"It was an experience I will likely never forget," Banju said, quoting Stonner's words.

"Good, good! Would you like to see the Rainbow Fountains now?"

"That would be great."

"Please, this way," he led them down a short pathway to one of the side streets. "Now the Rainbow Fountains were a gift from the elves during the reign of King Sagaxus himself. He had helped them solve a century-old dispute with the dwarves, you see." He continued to babble on, leading them through side street after side street until he finally stopped near the corner of a winery. "Gentlemen, around this corner is one of the most spectacular sights you will ever behold!"

They turned the corner into a central square bustling with activity. Vendors lined the walls of nearby buildings, desperately shouting at passersby about how grand their products were and why they should choose them. Hundreds of people were milling through the square, and only a handful paid these vendors any mind. A puppeteer was comically reenacting the Great King's battle with Narkk for a group of energetic, giggling children. In the dark shadows of the square stood the types of men who sold products as shady as their appearance. To their credit, they were acquiring the largest crowds yet.

All of these sights were obsolete, however, when Banju caught sight of the Rainbow Fountains on the other side of the square. Red, green, orange, blue, purple and other shades of the rainbow glowed in the water of each fountain that all came together into one swirling mixture in an octagonal pool in the center. Colorful glowing stones surrounded the fountains. At the center of the pool spouted one single spray with all of the colors of the rainbow in it. As they drew nearer, Banju saw that the colors of the stones at the bottom of the pool were not random, for they formed a wide tree that's roots and branches spread to each individual fountain. Inscribed on the walls behind it were colorful adaptations of the Great King's greatest triumphs, along with the elves' adaptations of Shallor's natural landmarks. A huge statue of Sagaxus stood over the proceedings.

"Magnificent, isn't it?" Matthew asked reverently.

Banju nodded in agreement, still too awed to speak.

"Believe it or not, this is nothing compared to the majestic Room of Jewels."

Curiosity brought Banju out of his trance. "Room of Jewels?"

"Aye, that's where the most important meetings are held in the palace. The stones and crystals there are believed to calm and focus the inhabitants of the chamber, resulting mostly in wise decision making."

"The elves certainly contributed a lot to this city."

"Indeed. Not only did they provide magical fountains or rooms, but they also helped our architects build Aldor. That's why most of the buildings are so tall and retain their clean color."

"I never thought of that," Stonner commented.

"Most people don't."

Though the rest of the tour was exciting and intriguing, Banju found it hard to focus; his mind kept wandering back to Kyron and the mission. How were they supposed to stop someone who had years of experience and escaped from a secure prison? They, who only months before, were living normal lives in their hometowns?

The tour eventually ended, and after graciously thanking Matthew, they headed for the city's central park. It was one of the only places aside from their chamber where they could think and clear their minds. They entered the huge park and continued to walk until they were in one of the thickest parts of the trees.

Once they sat on their favorite bench, Stonner picked up a stick and began to draw a diagram in the sand. After a few minutes, Banju could see that he was trying to construct a map of the area surrounding the banquet hall. He drew an x in the center of the map and drew arrows leading back to the x. Stonner sat as if contemplating his creation and then scribbled it out entirely. "This mission may be difficult," he remarked.

True Love?

The next day went by quickly for them; Vince came to their dorm again and gave them some final pointers on how to behave at the banquet and an update on their target. "Kyron has gathered a gang of criminals under his wing. We are not sure how many there are, but we are surprised that he has done this; it's not his style. Be on high alert tomorrow."

"Will do," Stonner said firmly. Once Vince left the room, he let out the breath that he had been holding. "So what do you think the chances of this guy actually being there are?"

"A thousand to one," Banju replied. "I'm going to go do some last minute reconnaissance around the city."

Stonner sat on one of the lounge chairs, hands to his stomach. "I think I'll stay and fill up. It's been a whole two hours since I ate last!"

Banju smiled and left for the streets. There were few places left to check, but there was one that they had somehow missed the first time around: a small, busy café not more than a hundred meters away from the banquet hall. He placed himself in front of it and used his hands as an aiming sight to evaluate the hall. He had a clear vantage point to one of the main windows; from this café someone could easily observe the banquet, or worse, fire a few precise arrows into their targets.

"What in the blazes are you doing?" someone said by his right.

He glanced to see who it was and his legs nearly faltered when he saw that it was a woman with a beauty unmatched by any other that he had ever seen. She had dark golden hair and light blue eyes. Those two alone were enough to enchant any man, but her well-balanced face sealed the deal. Despite the rest of her body being covered by a white blouse and black pants, he could tell that she was very slim and fit. She had her left hand on her hip and was eyeing him with criticism.

That is when he realized that he still had his hands pointed at the hall. He quickly put them behind his back and faced her. "Nothing of consequence. Why?"

She eyed him for a few more heart-skipping moments before answering, "You were just looking at the banquet hall as if you were sizing it up for an...an attack! You're not planning something, are you?"

"No, of course not! In fact, quite the opposite!"

She raised an eyebrow. "So you're palace security, then?"

"A knight," he corrected her as politely as he could.

"Really? You must have been knighted recently, then, because you're not as rude or overconfident as those other knights are. You part of the Prince's elite guard?"

He was surprised at her knowledge, but did not mind answering her questions. "One of the two thousand and five hundred who made it all the way through the trials."

She took a step toward him. "Impressive. Would you like to get a drink...um, what shall I call you?"

He searched his mind, trying to recall his name. "Banju, my lady," he replied. "And what may I call you?"

"Felicia. Now, Sir Banju, Victor of the Five Trials, would you like to escort me to this café and get a drink?"

He smiled at the way that she described him and offered her his arm. "It would be my honor, madam."

They sat at a two-person table that faced the banquet hall and the majestic palace beyond. A waiter soon came and took their orders of belh, a fruity tea that Banju had come to enjoy, and then they were by themselves. At least, Banju felt like they were, despite the noise coming from nearby tables. Never in his life had he been in a relationship with a woman, let alone one who asked *him* instead of the traditional man-asks-woman ways of the village. Of course, this drink could be nothing more than just that: a drink.

He wondered how he had been so lucky to spend time with someone so beautiful but figured it may only be because of his title.

She blushed as he stared into her never-ending eyes. "Forgive me; I do not mean to be so direct," he said.

Felicia smiled. "I don't mind. Most of the men I meet have sly tongues that hide what they really mean. But you," she put a hand gently on top of his, sending chills down his back, "you seem to be an honest man, Banju."

The waiter arrived with their beverages, and Felicia withdrew her hand. They sat for a moment in silence, sipping their belh.

Banju broke the silence first. "So, if you don't mind me asking: ever since I've arrived in this city I've noticed that every woman seems to wear a dress, skirt or something of the like; you are the first one I've seen dress differently. Why wear the blouse and pants instead of the usual dress attire?"

Her eyes became fiery and Banju could have sworn that he also saw a hint of rebellion in them. The red umbrella providing them shade cast an intense shade of orange on her hair, adding to her sudden ferocity. "Women have been labeled over the years as weak, petite people who are good for nothing more than housekeeping and..." She pounded a fist on the table and half-rose out of her seat, surprising Banju and the occupants of nearby tables. "...and pleasure!" She returned to her seat and slightly relaxed. "I'm trying to prove that that label is nothing but a false presumption! No, not *trying*; there's no need to try because few women of this day and age are like that! We can fight and lead just as well—if not better—as any man! But I don't need to explain myself to you, someone I barely know; you probably think that I'm crazy, don't you?"

"No, Felicia." He spoke as smoothly as he could to ensure her and the few curious onlookers that everything was all right. *Choose your words carefully.* "I think that you bring up a very logical case. I agree that there seems to be a cultural rift between men and women. There have been many arguments back home about this; my father was one of the leading figures in the debate. He said that the first step to peace must be equality. Now, women are being treated as equals. We already have a few female blacksmiths, grocers, traders; we even have a female lumberjack!"

Her eyes lightened and a small smile crept to her lips. "My, Banju, you *are* an interesting one. Where is home for you?"

He quietly sighed, happy to stray away from the hot topic. "Smith Village. It's far northwest; just about as close as you can get to the edge of the map without falling off."

She let out a small laugh. "I see. I live in Dunar with my father. He's a sailor, so the water-city is the perfect place for him."

"I hear that that place is built like a fortress. Is it true?"

"Nearly impenetrable by land; by water, if you can get past the archers, pikes, boulders and other barriers, you practically have the right to own the place."

"Do you like it there?"

Felicia sighed and took a sip of her belh. "If it was up to me, I would have left Dunar years ago. It smells like dead fish and moldy water. But my father's getting older and I can't possibly leave him there by himself. Luckily, the king requested that all available sailors go to his harbor for a 'top-secret mission,' whatever that means! So here I am in Aldor with my aunt while my father fulfills his wildest fantasies." She looked past the umbrella and up at the sun: almost noon. "Which reminds me: I have an appointment with her in just a few minutes." She rose. "I'm terribly sorry, Banju, but I must leave. Perhaps we'll meet again sometime."

"Sooner rather than later, I hope." He was then left alone with his thoughts and his drink. He regretted that their conversation had to be cut so short. *Right when our conversation was getting interesting, too. Could she be the one?*

Banju finished his tea and stood to leave but stopped when he noticed that someone in a black hood was standing where he had been just moments before observing the banquet hall. Banju caught his breath and slowly moved toward him.

To his surprise, the hooded man turned around and stared him right in the eyes. Banju nearly jumped when he saw that the man had a white lightning tattoo on the entire right side of his face. *Kyron!*

Kyron glared at him a moment longer, as if predicting Banju's intentions. He cockily saluted and then sprinted for the nearest intersection. Banju vaulted over the fence of the café in pursuit. A cart full of baskets blocked Kyron's path; he placed one foot on the moving back wheel and front-flipped over the entire cart, hitting the ground running. Banju, on the other hand, stopped and hopelessly watched as Kyron disappeared into the crowd.

How did he manage to pull that off? Stonner would not be happy.

Momentum

"You just let him escape?" Stonner exclaimed. "Why didn't you jump over the cart, too?"

"I might be fast, Stonner," Banju said, "but I'm not agile enough to pull something off like that."

Stonner began to pace, hands behind his back. "So you're saying that you can't do any sort of flip?" Banju nodded. "Well then, we're going to take care of that right now."

"Now?" Banju could not hide the hint of shock in his voice.

"Yes, now!" Stonner headed for the door. "Come: we are going to the park."

Stonner took him to a field with several scattered boulders of varying sizes. "Alright, here's what I want you to do: I want you to do a front-flip off of that boulder over there."

"You're starting me at *that* level?" Banju criticized. "Shouldn't I start off with something simpler and smaller?"

Stonner shook his head. "No, Banju, that would be the *easy* way out. You're hardly going to learn a thing that way. You must first conquer one of the hardest flips so that the easier ones will be no challenge for you."

Banju had a hard time accepting his logic but knew that resistance would be futile. "Alright, Stonner, you're the teacher. Can you show me how to do it first?"

"With pleasure," Stonner ran toward the rock, put his right foot on it, bent down to a ninety-degree angle, launched himself off the boulder, flipped and landed feet first on the ground. "See, Banju, not too bad, is it?"

"You know, I could break my neck if I do this wrong," Banju stated.

"You *could* break your neck doing a lot of things," Stonner persisted. "Just do the flip, Banju! Remember: momentum is everything!"

Banju sighed and ran toward the boulder. However, he hit it with a painful *thud*. As he lay on the ground, winded, Stonner said, "Alright, that was a good first try, but next time let's try actually running *on* the rock instead of *into* it."

A small crowd began to form around the field.

"Do I really have to do this in front of all these people?" Banju grumbled, getting back to his feet and holding his side.

"Absolutely! It will help you keep your pride in check!"

Banju failed several more times: slipping, sliding and hitting the ground and rock more times than he cared to remember. His shirt was soon soaked with sweat, and he removed it so that it would not hinder his efforts. His breathing became ragged and his body ached from the number of impacts. *I can do this; I would have had it the last time, but my back found the ground before my legs could.*

He prepped himself for his next attempt, ran full sprint toward and on the rock, threw his body forward with as much force as he could muster...and landed roughly on his right shoulder. Pain spread through his body like a virus and he felt the need to scream. The crowd roared with a sympathetic cry.

Stonner stood over him and offered a hand. "Perhaps we should stop before you hurt yourself further, Banju."

Banju was pulled to his feet, and the crowd began to quietly applaud when they saw that he was all right. "Perhaps we should, Stonner."

They returned to their dorm, Banju nursing his scrapes and bruises while Stonner continued to prepare for their impending mission.

The next day, they put on the richly fabricated black tunics that had come in the package. Vince had explained that this was the ideal apparel for their operation. Most of the knights attending the banquet would also be wearing black tunics, and black would be very effective if they had to chase Kyron out in the evening streets.

They walked up the marble steps of the banquet hall and were stopped by four armed men guarding the entrance. Only after stating their names and giving the guards their credentials were they allowed admittance.

Instantly they heard music playing and people talking merrily. Many crystal chandeliers hung from the ceiling, illuminating the hall with a yellowish-white glow. The hall was full of round tables topped with white cloths; a quarter of the hall had a checkered dance floor, a buffet and a stage where the musicians were playing. Each table had a bouquet of roses and lit candles on them, the combination of which caused a soothing smell to cling to the air. There were servers with silver platters that passed out champagne and delicious appetizers. From what Banju could tell, over five hundred people were attending the banquet.

"Ah! Banju and Stonner, over here!" Vince waved to them from a nearby table. When they arrived at the table, the people sitting there left and went to the dance floor. "No one has seen Kyron or any of his men yet," Vince murmured to them, casually grabbing a glass of champagne from a passing server. "My father is sitting at a table twenty paces behind us. He is being protected by the finest royal bodyguards, but I fear that if there is an attack, they won't be enough to stop Kyron from succeeding in whatever it is he has planned."

"If he tries anything, we'll be here to stop him," Banju assured.

Vince nodded gratefully. "I know." He stood. "Let me introduce you two to some of the important people of the kingdom."

Stonner shrugged. "Why not: we've got nothing better to do at the moment."

Acting as of he had not heard Stonner's sarcastic comment, Vince took them to a table occupied by only two men. "Banju, Stonner, this is Captain Pikt, First Officer in my father's military."

Captain Pikt was in his early fifties, had jet-black hair with streaks of white in it; cold, gray eyes and a dark, battle scarred face. When he stood up he was at least five inches taller than Banju. "I have heard a lot about you two," he shook their hands with a strong, firm grip, his voice low and strong. "It is a pleasure to finally meet you."

"The pleasure is all ours," Banju replied politely.

"If you two ever need anything, you just let me know."

"Thank you, sir, we'll keep that in mind," Stonner said with a smile.

The next man seemed to be in his mid-sixties, had white hair, blue eyes and was about the same height as Banju. "I am Lord Corbin of Cebil."

"It is a great pleasure to meet you, Lord Corbin," Stonner said.

"As it is a great pleasure to meet two legends like the two of you," Lord Corbin replied.

"Vinceterian! Vinceterian, are those your friends? Bring them over, if you please."

Vince sighed. "That would be my father. Care to meet him?" They nodded and followed him over to King Banton's table. "Father, why must you call me that? You know that I don't like it."

King Banton's eyes resembled Vince's, but his hair and beard were dark gray and it appeared that recent meals had not been kind to his weight. "It is your full name, is it not?" the king stated. "Who's ever heard of a child named 'Vince'?"

"Who's ever heard of a child named 'Vinceterian'?" Stonner interjected.

Banton chuckled. "You must be Stonner. Vince has told me a lot about you two. From what he's told me, you both have an impressive record in the tryouts. Congratulations on making knighthood, gentlemen."

"Thank you, King Banton," Banju said. "I'm sorry, but we really must be going."

"Of course, of course; we wouldn't want a terrorist taking action with you two off duty. Until next time, farewell."

With that, Banju and Stonner headed for their balcony that was fifteen meters above the dance floor, a perfect vantage point for them to monitor everyone there. "Anyone look suspicious?" Stonner asked as they neared the stairwell.

Banju quickly scanned the crowd of people. "Not that I can see thus far," he concluded.

"Banju!" a female voice called behind them. "Is that you?"

They turned, and Banju was shocked to see Felicia standing there, beautifully presented in a red silk dress and a red headband holding her braided hair in place. She smiled, and Banju felt the entire room suddenly shine brighter.

Stonner turned back around so she could not see him speak. "So *this* is the girl you went on and on about last night," he murmured and patted Banju's bruised shoulder. "Enjoy yourself, my friend; I'll go up onto the balcony and keep an alert eye out while you have yourself a dance."

Banju gratefully smiled, bowed and offered Felicia his hand. "May I have this dance, fair lady?" She took it and they began to dance to the elegant, slow song the musicians were playing. "What are you doing here? I mean, I'm happy you *are*, but why?"

"My aunt thought that it would be exciting to go to the king's ball and meet some eligible bachelors from the higher classes." She rolled her eyes. "I wouldn't be surprised if she isn't surrounded by dozens of them right now. Why are *you* here?"

"Personal request from the prince himself."

"Lucky you," she remarked.

They danced until the song was done and then Banju saw Stonner gesturing for him to come up. He gently grabbed Felicia by her shoulders and looked directly into her eyes, almost faltering as he did so. "Please listen to me, Felicia: find your aunt and get out of here as fast as you can."

She seemed perplexed. "Why, Banju? Is there something that you're not telling me?"

"Something bad is going to happen here, and I'm here to stop it," he said, "but I would never be able to live with myself if something happened to you tonight."

152

Felicia gazed into his eyes as if searching to see if he was bluffing. She relaxed and said, "Alright, Banju, I will go." She kissed him on the cheek. "And make sure that nothing happens to *you*, Sir Knight. See you around, I hope."

Once Banju climbed the stairs to their vantage point, Stonner said, "You've found a gem, my friend. Why does your face look so forlorn?"

"I told her to leave for her own safety," he replied. "This is the second time that our conversation has been brought to a close too soon."

"Well, that was probably the smartest thing that you could do for her. And don't worry: I'm sure you'll have a finer chance to talk with her longer another time." Stonner sighed, signifying that he was returning to the task at hand. "The only thing suspicious that I've seen so far is a server taking something from his own serving tray."

Banju grinned in agreement. The banquet was going smoothly: there were people dancing, chatting at the tables and eating. In his opinion, nothing else was going to happen that night.

That was when a gut wrenching feeling hit him, and he had only a second to react before the attack came. He pushed Stonner to the ground as an arrow whizzed by their former standing position.

Banju and Stonner sprang into action: Stonner stood back up with his bow in hand and Banju ran down the stairwell back into the hall. The hall went into chaos with people trying to run out of the building and others seeking cover. The arrow shot at Stonner was a diversion while a second arrow tried to hit the king; astonishingly, the arrow transformed into a blue bolt of lightning during its flight. Luckily (and unluckily), one of the king's bodyguards jumped in front of him and was hit instead. His body erupted into flame, and the blue fire spread to the nearby tables.

Banju searched for the shooter but was unable to find him in the sea of people. He glanced up at Stonner to see if he could identify the shooter but Stonner shook his head. Banju returned his attention back to the ground and saw a man concealed by a dark cloak stab someone, steal a ring of golden keys from the victim's belt, look straight at Banju and jump out of a stained-glass window.

Banju dashed after him, pushing past rows of screaming people and vaulting over tables. He jumped out the window and landed on the roof of a small shop. The moon lit his way as he followed the fugitive's trail. *Why take keys?* he wondered. Perhaps they unlocked a bank vault, or maybe they were the keys to prison cells. *Or they could be the keys to the gates to get out of the city.* Just as he was not certain, he was equally not sure that he wanted to know.

After there were no more clues as to where Kyron had gone, Banju stopped on the middle of a bridge. Unfortunately, this was a huge mistake, for dozens of men appeared and blocked him from getting off the bridge on either side.

"You're a smart man," the dark cloaked man from the banquet materialized out of the group of men in front of Banju. His voice was quiet and smooth with an eerie hint to it. "I've never had a more persistent pursuer. Whatever he has told you is most likely true, but you do not fully understand my position." He began to circle Banju as if trying to evaluate Banju's strengths and weaknesses. "All I want to do is leave this god-forsaken city and Shallor."

Banju slowly began to move his right hand inside his cloak for the throwing knives that he had hidden in it earlier. His aim was not as good as Stonner's, but he was still a decent shot. *I just need to stall him a little longer; I'm sure Stonner will be here soon.* "Then why make such a dramatic scene at the banquet?"

Kyron stopped in front of Banju. "Fear. It resides within us all. It hardens us, makes us turn against one another. It transforms even the most righteous of men into the vilest of monsters. And in the end, it is fear that we must overcome. This city is too peaceful; people have become indolent and content in this lie. I merely wanted to show them that chaos still exists." He started circling again. "And besides: what is it that great and powerful men fear the most? Losing their greatness."

Not much time; I need to act now. His hand had found the knives. "Perhaps you should have thought about that more before you lost your own greatness." He threw the knives in rapid succession at the men in front, drew Crikkon and charged the men behind him. Many of them he caught off guard, but there were a few who were prepared enough to put up a fight. They only took him a few more seconds to defeat, however.

Once he finished with them, he turned back around to see where Kyron was. Kyron was standing on the edge of one of the sides of the bridge. He smiled, his legendary silver tattoo glinting in the moonlight, and then flipped into the water below.

Banju sighed. *Here we go again.* He ran off of the bridge and followed Kyron on foot on the side of the river. Kyron stopped a hundred meters later and came out on the other side.

"You can't stop me," he shouted over the water.

Banju had one throwing knife left and smiled. "You underestimate me." He threw the knife and it hit Kyron in his left thigh.

Kyron grimaced and limped into the web of streets and buildings.

There was another bridge nearby, so Banju ran over it and went into pursuit. Now all he had to do was follow the small trail of blood, which was rather difficult to see in the darkness. The trail of blood stopped abruptly below a ladder leading up to the roof of a tall building. Banju began to climb up, noticing little dark red marks on the ladder.

The building was well over ten stories high, and Banju only wished that he didn't have to fight at the top of a building so high. *So many things could go wrong.* Another thought crossed his mind. *Where was Stonner?*

As he was nearing the top, he could see Kyron climbing up the final length of the ladder. Banju's arms and legs were fatiguing. When he reached it, he stopped abruptly. Kyron was standing on the other side of the flat roof, aiming his loaded bow at Banju. "Remove the cloak slowly," he ordered.

Banju dropped his cloak, leaving him in his dark tunic and his only weapon now being Crikkon. "I can help you," Banju suggested. "I can mend your wound and you'll return to prison unharmed."

Kyron chuckled. "This wound is nothing; I can mend it myself." He dropped the bow. "They'll never let me return to prison now; they would rather kill me than put me back there. I know too much."

Banju shook his head. "You don't know that."

Kyron nodded and slowly approached him. "I know very well what will happen. The fire has started, and it won't stop until it has consumed all of Shallor." He removed his cloak, revealing the knife still lodged in his left thigh. His tattoo glimmered once more in the moonlight. "But as you can see, I'm a fair man. I could have killed you when you first came up here." He put his left hand on the curved hilt of his sword. "A fight to the death, a fight for freedom."

Banju unsheathed Crikkon and stood in a defensive stance. "You're making a big mistake; I could help you."

"I don't think so; besides, I would rather die at the hands of an honorable man like you than at the hands of cruel executioners. But," he drew his weapon in a flash, "I will not be the one dying today."

He struck in a quick, wide upper arc that Banju just barely deflected. Banju tried to move to the center of the roof while blocking a barrage of brutal attacks. Kyron feigned to the right and struck to the left, and Banju parried as swiftly as he could.

The battle was over just as quickly as it had begun when Kyron locked blades with Banju, punched him in the jaw and kneed him in the gut. Banju fell, unable to breathe or cry out in pain.

Kyron stood above him, his sword pointed cautiously by Banju's right leg. "You put up a good fight; most men only last a few seconds. Goodbye, my persistent pursuer." He raised the blade to decapitate Banju's head.

Banju was going to react by rolling to the side, thus tripping Kyron and regaining Crikkon, but was unable to before two arrows buried themselves in Kyron's chest. The fugitive gasped, dropped his sword, stepped back a few paces and jumped off of the ten-story building.

After a few moments of shocked silence, a blue streak of lightning flashed in the night sky and Banju sat up and looked over the edge. Down below, he could just make out the silhouette of Kyron's body in the street. He looked back to see who had fired and saw Stonner on the roof of a building nearby. Banju breathed a sigh of relief and began a slow, painstaking climb back down the ladder.

When he reached ground level, Stonner and Vince were waiting for him. "Well done, Banju," Vince congratulated. "If it wasn't for you, we never would have stopped Kyron."

Banju nodded groggily. "Thank you, sir." He looked around for Kyron's body. "Kyron?"

"We had someone pick his remains up for proper burial," Stonner replied.

"Good work again, you two," Vince said. "Get some rest and I'll be in touch with you shortly on our *real* mission."

Once Vince had left, Banju and Stonner began to walk back to their chamber. "You did very well today, Banju," Stonner said. "I would've been there sooner if I hadn't been stopped by a score of criminals on a bridge who seemed to have just woken from a fitful sleep." He looked at Banju. "Is something wrong?"

"Besides the obvious fact that I am still getting over the thrill of the chase, I was wondering: Why shoot him in the chest? Why not just immobilize him?"

Stonner became grim. "I had a moment to react. I had just reached the top of the building when I saw him raise his sword to kill you. And then…" He paused as realization sunk in. "I did not expect him to *jump*."

Banju let him sulk for a few minutes before saying, "There is one more thing that bothers me."

"And what is that?"

"What in Shallor were those keys for?" They both chuckled to lighten the mood as they walked down the street to their dorm.

A War to Be Fought

After the trying events of the last few days, Vren invited Banju and Stonner to join him and a handful of other new knights at a tavern to celebrate their rise to knighthood. They graciously accepted.

The tavern was located in a secluded portion of Aldor, but it was difficult to compare it to any other tavern once they entered. A plaque inscribed *The Red Goat* was set above the door; a large stuffed goat dyed red stood erect over the bar. Lanterns hung from rafters, and a mirror behind the bar gave the small tavern the illusion that it was twice its size. As the new knights found a table, the tavern keeper—a man with a rough complexion but kindly eyes—approached with a tray of filled mugs. "A round on me for our kingdom's hope!"

The men cheered, and a bard in the corner began to sing,

> *Our kingdom's hope, our kingdom's hope!*
> *How everything's simpler to uncoiled rope!*
> *Share a drink, clink, clink, clink,*
> *For the soon-to-be heroes.*
> *Dreams of valor, dreams of strength,*
> *Dreams devoid of swords and arrows;*
> *Let them have these dreams for some length,*
> *For they are our kingdom's hope!*
> *So break a keg! Share a drink!*
> *Clink, clink, clink!*

Banju raised his mug to his lips but stopped when he saw his father in the mirror's reflection. He was smiling, the way he always had when Banju had done something to make him proud. Banju blinked, and his father disappeared. Disheartened, he put his mug down. Stonner, Vren and the others chugged their drinks and laughed airily as they asked for more.

Turning to leave the tavern, Banju spotted Vince sitting at a corner table alone, his face distraught and a bottle of half-gone wine in his hands.

"Vince, are you alright?" Banju asked him, unsure why the royal prince would be in a tavern such as this.

"Ah, Banju, I see that you and the other knights are enjoying yourselves." Vince's voice was thick with wine. "Would that I could do the same. Please, sit."

"Is all well?"

Vince snorted. "Is it? I have lost all sense to discern whether 'tis or 'tisn't. I'm sure you mean to ask, 'Why are you here, my prince? Shouldn't you be drinking at your palace?'" He chuckled and sipped from the bottle. "Do you know why my father had the Five Trials?"

"I assumed that it was to train a force of men so that we may conquer Makir," Banju said carefully.

A gleam of despair entered Vince's eyes. "Aye, but that is not the only reason." He drank more wine and set it down with a *clunk*. "My father...my father wanted to keep me occupied. He wanted to test me…to see if I could handle a command. You see, he doesn't love nor trust me."

Banju wanted to object, but the words did not come, and Vince continued in a melancholy tone, "I wasn't his first son, nor was I ever the son that he wished to have. *Peter*, that's who he wanted to be his heir. Firstborn and noble-hearted, Peter impressed my father and mother at a young age. He was a brilliant swordsman and words flowed off of his tongue like rich honey; or so they tell me. At the age of ten, Peter came down with a terrible illness and died. My father and mother's dreams were shattered in that moment, and they never fully recovered.

"However, they decided to try to have a son once more, so that the future of the kingdom would be secured. Enter Vinceterian." Vince thrust a thumb at himself. "I am told that I gave my mother much pain during the labor process; she passed away soon after my birth. His favorite son and loving wife gone, my father despairingly settled for me. He still blames me for her death, though, and doesn't believe that I will ever live up to Peter's potential." His tale complete, Vince swigged more wine.

"Vince, I—"

"I do not ask for your sympathy, Banju; I only wish for you to understand…" His face became befuddled, and his eyes began to glaze over. "What is it that I wanted you to understand? I seem to have forgotten." Vince's head began to droop. "I suppose it is rather late; perhaps…perhaps I should get some sleep." He rested his head on the table.

Banju stood. "Good night, my prince. I hope that peace will find you in your dreams."

After informing Vince's guards standing outside of the prince's condition, Banju headed for his dorm, his mind churning with all that he had just learned.

A week passed without any word from Vince or anyone else. Banju began to worry that the prince had sunk into a pit of despair just as Banju had after his father's death. To pass the time and ease their anticipation, Banju and Stonner would get up every morning and run laps around their favorite location: the central park. Not only was it good exercise, but it was also a great way for them to briefly forget about the Kyron incident.

"Do you think something's wrong?" Banju asked Stonner one day.

Stonner shook his head. "No, he's probably too busy what with Kyron's death and all. Don't worry; I'm sure he'll contact us soon."

"You're probably right." Banju had kept Vince's tale to himself; Stonner was none the wiser.

Later in the week they received a note that read,

Central park. Noon. Important.

~P.V.

Intrigued, Banju and Stonner entered the park around noon; they followed the main path, but after several minutes, they began to fear that the prince was not coming. As if on cue, they saw Vince waving just ahead on the twisted path. When he reached them, he inquired: "Do you two know of a quiet place where we can speak?"

"We have just the spot," Stonner replied. He led Vince to their favorite bench near the center of the park.

"Very convenient," Vince observed as he sat down and looked up at the canopy of trees above them. "I am sorry to keep you two waiting for so long; there were some things I had to do behind the scenes with my father. And Banju," he looked at him with a mysterious glint in his eye, "I apologize for my behavior the other night. No one should ever have to see their prince in such a state."

Banju bowed his head. "There is nothing to apologize for, my prince. I only hope that you have recovered from your ordeal."

Stonner watched on confused, but didn't say a word. "I have," Vince replied with a small smile. "Now I must be blunt: my father has decided that we must strike against Makir immediately."

"What?" Stonner asked disbelievingly. "In the blink of an eye, we are at war?"

"And why now," Banju insisted, "why not years ago when our forces were stronger and we had more men?"

Vince glanced around to make sure no one else was listening. Banju noted that he seemed to be doing that a lot lately. "Back in the day when we had more men, Makir was not a huge threat to us. However, for the past two hundred years, a silent war has been waged between us and them; a war of words, espionage and rumors. But now, things have changed drastically: they have found the Golden Gauntlet."

Banju's breath caught in his throat. The gauntlet that could control nature, create living beings, had been *found*.

Stonner recovered enough from the news to ask, "How long have they had it in their possession?"

"Our informants believe that Sarkk—the ruler of Makir now—discovered it over five months ago."

"So he's had over five months to create an army of his wildest imaginings," Banju thought aloud.

"Yes," Vince concurred. "That is what we believe, and that is why we must attack as soon as possible. We have an entire fleet going to Makir in two week's time; I hope that you two will accompany us."

"Magic gauntlet or not, we're with you," Banju said.

"Aye," Stonner added thoughtfully.

Vince smiled and stood up to leave. "Good; the troops will be gathering at the east gate in two weeks to depart. See you then, gentlemen."

"Just one more thing," Stonner interjected.

Vince stopped and faced Stonner. "Yes?"

"This has been bothering me for days now," Stonner said, thumbs twiddling, "What were those keys that Kyron tried to steal?"

Vince smiled and continued to walk away. "That is classified information, Stonner; you're going to have to ask me again after we return from Makir."

ooo

Hearts of Fire and Crimson

On the third day of their hunt, Rik and the others reached Woodsbane. Black trees contrasted with the green mountains beyond them, and the forest was silent save for the rustling of leaves and the occasional call of an unfamiliar bird. An eerie presence was palpable in the air, as if someone or something was watching the Horizon Guard's every move.

Two hundred yards within, Knip dismounted and knelt to draw his hands along the ground. "It's passed through here recently."

"How long?" Captain Bree inquired.

Knip knitted his brows and pensively bit his lip. "No more than half a day ahead of us, sir."

Captain Bree looked above them at the tangled overhanging branches. "We have only a few hours before nightfall. Keep an eye out for an ideal campsite; 'twould be suicide to continue the hunt in the dark in a forest such as this."

The forest began to close in around them. As the shadows lengthened, Warren directed them to a circular cluster of disfigured oaks. Knip and Ross heatedly debated whether to light a fire or not, and they would have continued bantering for several minutes if Bree had not said, "A fire may draw unwanted attention, but several of Woodsbane's inhabitants are likely not used to seeing such light at night and will try to avoid it."

With that settled, they prepared for a slim dinner of jerky and the last loaf of bread from their village replenishments. The tense silence throughout revealed to Rik that the others were just as uneasy as he was. Darkness settled in; the wind howled and the trees swayed as if they were alive. From the mound of moss that he was sitting on, Rik could still see the red and green tracks glowing on the path.

"What do we do if it doubles back and attacks us?" His question seemed to stir the others out of their dread-filled trances.

"You have probably realized by now that each of us has a specific skill…" Ross smiled and tapped his nose. "Mine happens to be setting traps. Before we retire for the night, I plan to put nets between the trees and other traps that will warn us if anything gets too close. In fact, I should probably do that now." He rose and headed for his saddlebag.

"Surround us with the horses while you're at it," Bree ordered. "Their heightened senses will act as our night watchers." To Rik he asked, "You do know how to fight, correct?"

"My father is a blacksmith," Rik replied. "I have known how to use a sword since I was old enough to hold one."

Brack threw another log on the fire and gave him a sorrowful glance.

Knip chuckled emptily. "Brack knows a thing or two about swordplay; he danced with death more than once during his days in Makir." Seeing the look of awe and shock on Rik's face, he explained, "Brack here was born and raised in the smokes of Makir. If you're lucky enough, he'll let me share his tale."

At first Brack only glared into the fire with his golden eyes. It reminded Rik of melting gold. Nets were now encompassing the weak spots in the campsite; their dark green complexion blended with the drooping foliage of the trees' twisted and intertwined limbs. The air was cold enough to see one's breath in, and Rik wrapped his cloak more firmly about him and inched closer to the fire. It was as he did so that Brack nodded.

"As Brack would tell you, this is not his first encounter with magic," Knip began. "He was born in Makir which is known among other things for still being rampant with magic. Lords like to say that they are in control, but it is really the slavers and wizards who command the land. In a land of disorder, the larger cities act as their own governments, and the smaller villages must pay tribute to them for fear of being obliterated." Knip absentmindedly traced his fingers through the dirt; behind him, Ross could be seen concealing a noose on the trail. "It was within such a village that our dear Brack was born. As time went on and he grew stronger, Brack decided to raise his village against tyranny."

Brack kept his eyes on the flames, but Rik noted that tears were forming. Knip continued, "His noble heart sought the support of the surrounding villages, but no aid came. The cities soon fell upon him and massacred the town, killing all...all, save Brack. He was taken to the ruins of Narkk's castle to be made an example of for any others who wished to be heroes. A wizard met him there and declared that his punishment for speaking against the rulers was eternal silence." Knip rubbed his throat. "The wizard destroyed Brack's vocal cords with a single malicious spell...He was to be sold into slavery after that, but the slave caravan was intercepted by a man who rescued Brack. This man did not tell Brack his name, but he helped him overtake a sloop and urged him to travel to the noble land of Shallor." His story drawing to a close, Knip cracked his knuckles. "And that is when my brother and I came across Brack. We joined the Horizon Guard together, and he relayed his past to us through written word."

Unsure what to say afterward, Rik only said, "I'm sorry, Brack."

Brack broke his gaze on the fire, grabbed a stick and wrote in the earth: *NO NEED FOR PITY.*

Captain Bree sighed. "Well I've heard enough despairing tales for one night. Let's get some sleep."

Rik grabbed two fur blankets and lay down on soft moss by the fire, his mind swirling with heart-eating monsters and sorcerers who ripped out vocal cords again and again. He would have descended deeper into his nightmares if not for the crashing sound of a tree halfway through the night. At first he did not know what to make of it, but realization soon dawned on him: *One of Ross's traps has caught something!* Someone yelled nearby, and Rik jumped out of his furs, his two-and-a-half-foot sword in hand.

The campsite was in disarray; the timbers from the fire pit had been spread apart, lighting the captain's tent and the surrounding branches ablaze. Ross's nets were torn and his nooses hung empty. Two horses lay writhing on the ground in their death throes. Knip, Ross and Brack were battling a coyote-like stone creature while Bree and Warren were fighting another. After a moment's hesitation, Rik ran to Bree and joined in the fray.

He sliced at the creature's tail; its skin was as hard as rock, and his sword only managed to cut a half an inch into the beast. Nevertheless, the stone monster yelped and kicked Rik with its hind legs, sending him winded to the ground. Warren and Bree tried their best to combat the brute, but their swords kept bouncing harmlessly off of its granite armor. The creature's tail began to bleed green. It was not long before the stone coyote snarled and leapt at Warren; its claws ripped into his chest, taking bone and flesh with it as it withdrew. Warren collapsed, blood spurting in a thousand different directions. Recovered, Rik threw a flaming log at the beast's chest. The log reflected off of its hide, but it seemed to be frightened by the heat. Thinking quickly, Rik grabbed another and intercepted the monster. It bristled and pounded its front legs into the ground, but it did not advance; instead, it turned and ran into the dark forest. Rik laughed with the thrill of adrenaline pounding through him.

However, he froze when he turned and saw that another stone coyote had leapt out of the woods and knocked over Bree. The captain screamed as the creature put all of its weight on his legs and came in for the kill. Rik tried to tell himself to move, to help Bree, but his arms and legs would not cooperate. Just as the beast was about to bite Bree's throat, Brack jumped out of nowhere, raised his spear-axe-sword and brought it down with all of his might on the creature's neck. For one gut-wrenching moment it seemed as if the weapon had had no effect, but then the creature stopped snarling and the top part of its head split and became parallel with its chest, sending pools of green blood onto the captain.

The fight was over, and they had won.

Knip and Ross pushed the beast off of Bree. He coughed and said, "Don't worry about me; focus on Warren."

"We tried," Ross offered. "He was dead before we reached him."

Rik glanced over at the punctured body of his companion. *Best prepare for the worst,* Warren had said. *It may be the only difference between life and death.* Even the worst could not have prepared them for this.

"We must…follow the one that escaped. It will lead us to its master," their captain ordered.

Knip glanced at Bree's legs. "Your legs are crushed; you are in no condition to continue the hunt."

Moving to a sitting position, Bree swore. "We cannot let this evil thrive unchallenged. You four must follow this mission through to the end."

Ross shook his head. "My brother and I will stay here with you. If one of those things returns, you won't be able to defend yourself."

"Then Rik, Brack, it is up to you," Bree said.

As stunned as he was, Rik managed to solemnly nod. He turned to leave, but Bree grabbed his sleeve. "Rik, you must not freeze like that again, understood?"

"Yes, captain."

Bree sat back and closed his eyes. "Dunar and all Shallor rest on your shoulders. Remember that, and be smart."

With that, Rik gathered his bow and arrows, and he and Brack descended into the dark foliage. The beast had left an easily visible trail in its wake; plants were split, tree limbs were snapped and green blood smeared the ground. Rik gripped his bow tighter to ease his anticipation.

The trees began to thin, and Rik and Brack entered an eerie field at the foothills of the Smith Mountains. The wind howled at them like wraiths, and the gray grass writhed as if it were a sea of snakes. By the moon's pale light, Rik observed that their prey's tracks were becoming closer together and more erratic. *We are getting close.*

Sure enough, they found the creature at the mouth of a shadowy cave; it had bled out from the wound that Rik had inflicted, and it lay in a twisted position. "Have you seen these monsters before, Brack?" Rik whispered to him, as if fearing that the beast would revive at the sound of his voice.

Brack nodded and scribbled something into the ground with his spear-axe-sword: *BRAEESH.*

The braeesh's snout faced the cave, and Rik quietly debated whether to investigate it or not. Seeing his companion's conflictions, Brack clasped his shoulder with a hand twice as big as Rik's, pointed at the entrance and nodded.

"We don't know what we'll find in there; I'll enter with bow drawn, and you follow close behind me in case we are attacked, alright?" Another nod, and they headed into complete darkness. Fifty sweat-soaked steps later, Rik's eyes grew accustomed enough for him to make out the dark shapes of the cavern's walls. No sounds could be heard save their tense breathing and the light footfalls of Brack behind him. However, two hundred steps in, Rik could hear a slow, faint, reverberating echo: *thump-thump, thump-thump, thump-thump.* A reddish-gold light appeared in a tunnel up ahead. Rik's nerves churned in his stomach as they neared the light. *Thump-thump, thump-thump, thump-thump.* Only a few steps more;

he dropped to a crouch and raised his bow. *Thump-thump, thump-thump, thump-thump.*

They entered the lit tunnel. Ten yards in, it opened and descended into a huge cavern. Rik signaled for Brack to follow him to an outcropping of stalagmites as he scouted the area. Below them, Rik witnessed a supernatural sight that made him catch his breath in awe: the cavern was circular, went on for at least three hundred feet and was filled with hundreds of crimson-skinned human-like creatures that slept on stone slabs two feet apart. *Thump-thump, thump-thump, thump-thump.* At the cavern's center Rik found the sound's source—scores of still-beating hearts pulsated in a giant goblet. *Thump-thump, thump-thump.* A man garbed in a gold and silver robe held a heart in his hand and spoke to it in an unknown language.

This must be the darkest of magics. Rik drew his bowstring back, aimed for the man's head and fired. The arrow shot through the air in utter silence, but somehow it came to an abrupt halt inches from the sorcerer. The man faced Rik and swirled a finger in the air; Rik found himself lifted by invisible hands and thrown roughly down the slope.

"Who are you?" the sorcerer demanded as he approached Rik. His hair was long and burned a fiery orange; his skin was pale and slightly wrinkled and his eyes were a mismatched dark purple and icy blue. "Did Fayn send you?"

Rik pushed himself up. His bow had fallen ten feet to his right, but he still had his sword. "I do not know what you are talking about."

The man grimaced and began to choke Rik with invisible hands. "Speak to me truly, and I may not rip your heart out for the sacrifice." He shoved the heart in his hand at Rik's face for emphasis. "These are Malen's warriors now; Fayn has waited too long."

Rik glanced at the steady rise and fall of the nearest creature's large chest. *Thump-thump, thump-thump, thump-thump.* "What...what are these things?"

Malen looked at him with dismay. "You really don't know, do you? How unfortunate." He walked back to the goblet, and Rik found himself unwillingly following. Malen cast the heart in with the others. "The words have been said; now all that remains is to offer my blo—"

Rik had unsheathed his sword and tried to strike Malen, but an unseen shield deflected his blow, and orange bolts sent Rik flying into the nearest sleeper. The creature did not react, and Rik recovered and charged at Malen. The sorcerer waved his hand, and another sleeper crashed into Rik. The body was heavier than Rik had expected, and he found that it trapped him from his left arm down. He desperately tried to escape from under it as Malen drew near.

Thump-thump, thump-thump, thump-thump.

"I see that I must kill you," Malen said. "Such a pity for one so young. Your heart will help strengthen my army as we conquer Shallor." Malen's right hand reached for Rik's chest; there was a slicing sound, and Malen's arm was no longer there. As Malen contemplated this turn of events, Brack appeared at his side. Malen shot out a blast of orange energy, but Brack swiftly dodged it and swiped with his spear-axe-sword; Malen's body collapsed as his head left his body.

The deed done, Brack easily lifted the sleeper off of Rik. "Thank you, Brack," Rik man-aged to say as he grabbed his bow. "Now we need to decide what to do about these creatures."

Brack pointed at a torch, and Rik caught his meaning as clear as day. He slung his bow, acquired two torches and headed for the giant goblet. *Thump-thump, thump-thump, thump-thump.* Rik dropped the torches into the sea of hearts. *Thump-thump-thump-thump-thump-thump.* To his surprise, all of the sleepers moaned and their bodies thrashed. *Thump-thump-thump-thump.* The hearts were consumed in flames; the sleepers stopped moving and the hearts could no longer be heard.

Despite his shock, Rik turned and headed for the tunnel, ever-suspicious that one of the creatures would wake up and attack him. They made it out of the cave, and Rik was relieved to see the sun rising above the treetops.

"Come on; we should make sure that Captain Bree is alright," he said to Brack. "But first we should block off this entrance. We don't want someone else finding…whatever it is that's down there."

Brack climbed high above the entrance and struck the rocky slope. Within minutes he sent huge chunks of rock cascading down upon the cave. No one would be entering or exiting that cave any time soon.

Reassured, Rik and Brack began to retrace their steps through the untamed forest.

○○○

From Ruins to Storms

"Are you ready, Stonner?" Banju asked as he stood impatiently by the door to their chamber.

There was a *thud* and then Stonner walked out with several satchels hanging around his shoulders. "I'm ready now."

Banju laughed as they strolled down the long corridor. "Why did you pack so many things? We're going on a warship, not a luxury cruise!"

"Half is for the journey to the harbor," Stonner explained. "The other is for our voyage."

They got on horses provided by Vince and traveled down the main street with the rest of the parade of knights where rows of people were uproariously cheering them on. Thousands of knights filled the street for several city blocks. Banju felt proud to be riding alongside some of the best knights in the kingdom—some of them twice his age and experience. After a few minutes of adjusting to the cheering and overwhelming feelings flooding him, he decided to follow the knights' gestures and smiled and waved at the crowd.

By noon they had reached the eastern gate, a huge arch hidden in the face of a small mountain at the back of the city. Banju remembered hearing that this gate was once shrouded in secrecy and originally built as an escape route in case the city was ever lost in a siege; now it was used as a shortcut to get to the harbor.

The first five miles were through a red-lit tunnel that went under the small mountain and came out near a waterfall on the other side. Once through, a deep green valley and thousands of tall trees surrounded them. According to one of the knights riding by Banju, it would take them over three days to cross over the entire valley. *Pretty big valley,* he thought in amazement.

It took him a while to notice that there were many ruins strewn throughout the valley. One he identified as an ancient castle, another looked like a cathedral, but others were damaged so considerably by the ravages of time that they were beyond recognition. He guessed that this valley was likely the resting place of an ancient city from hundreds, maybe thousands, of years ago. When he asked some of the knights about it, a number of them would spit on the ground and say that the place was cursed and was still haunted by the ancient city's deceased inhabit-ants. Others would just shrug and say they had no idea what the city used to be and how it had been destroyed. There was one knight, however, who told him that he believed that the ancient city used to be inhabited by Drifters until the Fall of the Golden Age when the Drifters were forced to extinction.

After that Banju stopped asking questions and observed how the setting sun's rays seemed to hit the archaic castle perfectly and its steeples appeared to glisten with their own light. He did not know if it was a coincidence or if the castle had been built in that specific location for that purpose. *I may never know for sure what this place used to be or what its purpose was,* he mused.

Once the sun had gone down, they stopped and set up camp several miles away from the ruins as if they feared that the ghost stories were true.

He did not have much time to ponder, though, for he had to find Stonner so they could pitch their tent. Luckily, Banju found him in a very short amount of time. "Strange ruins, eh?" Stonner asked.

"Aye," Banju answered. "What were almost more peculiar were the responses I received when I asked questions about them."

"Indeed; not many people want to talk about it."

Once they had put their gear within the tent, a messenger respectively stood without. "Is there something I can help you with, sir?" Stonner inquired.

"The prince wishes for you two captains to be present for the battle briefing," the messenger replied. "Please, follow me."

The briefing tent was a huge pavilion near the center of the camp and was occupied by over a hundred knights, captains, generals and lords. Near the back, King Banton and Vince stood by a huge map of Shallor, Makir and the ocean that separated them.

"Welcome, gentlemen," the king began, "our plan is simple, but may be difficult to fulfill." He grabbed a dagger and circled several areas of Makir. "Each ship will land in different locations throughout Makir and will have the objective of destroying each and every city or town you come across, thus cutting off any means of reinforcements. Once we accomplish this, we will all merge on the castle itself to end this war!" The tent was filled with applause.

Once the applause ended, one of the captains said, "My king, is it true that there is a beast that guards the waters near Makir?"

Captain Pikt stepped forward and laughed. "That is only a sailor's tale, my boy! No beast could stop our great armada from reaching Makir; not even the Creator could stop us now!"

However, Banju did not clap nor laugh; for reasons unknown to him, he asked, "My king, is it truly necessary to massacre each and every city?"

One of the lords near King Banton was appalled. "You dare to speak against your king, knight?"

The king raised a hand, his face expressionless. "Enough, Nieg. I did not call this war council so that you would all thoughtlessly accept my plan. Tell me, Sir Banju, what you would have us do."

"Imagine…" Banju cleared his throat. "Imagine if we were being attacked instead. Millions of us would instantly attempt to defend our land. If our assailants were victorious, should they put us all to the sword? In the same way, does all of Makir deserve to be punished for the sins of their ruler? Certainly, we will meet some resistance from the townsfolk, but many of them will only be defending their homes and the land that they know, just as we would. I suspect that there are thousands of men, women and children who would stand against Sarkk. I propose giving these citizens the chance to surrender and come back with us to Shallor."

The assembly was tensely quiet; King Banton tugged on his beard before replying, "You took a gamble speaking out, and I respect that; you voiced one of my own doubts." He then addressed the entire pavilion, "The man who does not give Makir's inhabitants this opportunity will be stripped of all honors and privileges. Any other questions or suggestions? Good. Let us return to our tents and find rest."

"That was quite a noble thing you did," Stonner said as he and Banju walked back to their tent in the darkness of night.

"It felt odd opposing the king."

Stonner opened one of the tent's flaps and held it so Banju could step in first. Once they lit a lantern, he asked, "Do you think it's true?"

"What?"

Stonner casually grabbed a banana from his overfilled satchel. "That a monster guards Makir's waters."

Banju shrugged. "I don't think so. Why? Are you afraid of sea monsters?"

Stonner chuckled awkwardly. "Afraid of sea monsters? I have no fear of them; what would give you such an absurd idea?"

Banju smiled and dropped the subject because he was too tired to continue bantering. His legs and back were aching from extensive horse riding. He was about to ask Stonner how he felt but then saw that he had already fallen asleep: a half-eaten banana still in his hand, the other half sticking out of his mouth. Banju smiled, lay back and blew out the lantern.

Soon they would be on a ship and Banju could not help but admit that he was a little apprehensive himself. It would be his first time on a ship and the first time on the rough high seas. He was sure it would not be too bad, but what if the ship sank? There would be no hope then, for Vince had told them that each ship would be miles apart from each other to ensure their forces would land at the proper locations. *The best thing to do is pray and hope that we don't crash.*

They woke early the next morning extremely sore, packed up their things and continued on their journey to the harbor. By midday they were near the top of the valley. Banju regretted not being able to stay longer; he would have liked to look at the ruins more closely. He quietly promised that someday he would return and visit the ruins in finer detail.

They passed through a small ravine that opened up into the long path that would eventually take them to their destination. Today Banju had the lucky chance to ride by Vince and talk with him more about their coming battle.

"I want you and Stonner on separate ships so that if anything goes wrong, either one of you will take action for the sake of the crew," Vince informed him. "You will be accompanying General Valerin and Stonner will be accompanying Captain Malco. They are both honorable and wise men; I think that you will like Valerin."

"Sir, it has been bothering me." Banju repositioned the reigns on his horse. "Why us? I mean, why give us special treatment? Why did you choose us for that covert mission, and why choose us to be second in command on the vessels we will be voyaging on?"

Vince smiled. "Mostly because you two are two of the best warriors that I've ever seen. There is something about the two of you, Banju—as if each of you knows what the other is planning at any given moment." He briefly glanced up at the sky to watch the coming storm clouds. "I chose you as second in command of the ships because you both have leadership skills and the ability to make decisions independently without orders being given. Also, if you two see anything wrong you will most likely leap immediately into action, as you proved last night."

Banju nodded and was about to reply when a loud clap of thunder shook the air. "Ah, we don't have much more time," Vince observed. "There is a small town about three miles away; that's where we're going to stop for the night."

Small is an overstatement, Banju thought. The town was half a mile in diameter and only had a few dozen houses and public buildings within the village limits. The town was so small, apparently, that it was not on any maps and the inhabitants had never bothered to name it. He noticed that portions of the town were in ruins, seeming to be the outcome of a recent attack.

The knights were greeted by silence as the inhabitants of the small town watched them set up camp along its perimeter. Banju noted that most of them wore sad expressions and tattered clothing. He went over to Stonner who was beginning to once again pitch their tent.

"Do you notice anything strange about this village?" Banju asked him.

Stonner nodded and hammered one of the stakes into the ground. "The town looks as if it just survived a siege and the citizens seem to not be pleased that we are here."

"What do you say that after we pitch the tent we go into town and find out what has happened?"

"Agreed."

The storm was nearly upon them by the time they had finished assembling their tent. The entire horizon was filled with a black wall of storm clouds that seemed like an abyss that consumed all light.

Banju and Stonner headed into the pitiful town; thunder rumbled in the distance. They entered what looked like a tavern, and inside a dozen men sat and watched them suspiciously as they sat at a table in the corner.

"Can I help you, gentlemen?" the bartender asked in a gruff voice.

"We came here for answers," Banju replied. "The question is, sir: Can *we* help *you*?"

A burly man who sat at the bar snorted and chugged down his mug of beer. "What can you possibly do for us? You royal knights have no time to 'elp the likes of us! You're too busy polishin' your armor and findin' ways to look good in the public eye."

"Shut up, Toreh," the man next to him growled. "Maybe these knights are different; maybe they'll help us."

The first man laughed and coughed at the effort. "What help will they be? If we couldn't stand up to 'em, what makes you think that these two'll make a difference?"

"Because we *are* different," Stonner said as he moved to the bar. "We specialize in solving problems. Now are you going to tell us how we can help, or are we going to waste time arguing?"

The second man gestured to Toreh to be silent. "We recently have suffered many attacks from a group of brigands who fancy themselves to be raiders. When they first found our village, they offered us protection from other evils, in exchange for a 'small fee.' We agreed, but now I see in hindsight that we should've refused right then and there. Not that that would've done us much good. As time went on, their demands grew more and more until we had to struggle to pay them. Apparently that wasn't enough, for they began to raid us a few weeks back, taking livestock, families, supplies and whatever else they could get their filthy hands on. Now they are toying with us; it is only a matter of time before they come in for the kill."

Toreh spat. "Their leader, a man with an iron finger, took ma wife an' kids an' tol' me 'e was gonna kill 'em unless I paid 'im three 'undred gold."

"An iron finger?" Banju asked. Memories flashed through his mind as he remembered his fateful journey to Aldor. "Was it in place of his right index finger?"

Toreh nodded. "Aye."

Banju took Stonner aside. "Stonner, I think that this is the same group of bandits who attacked me on my way to Aldor."

"What are the odds of that happening?" Stonner murmured. "Are you sure?"

Banju addressed Toreh and the rest of the men. "Do they have a camp nearby?"

"Aye," the second man replied. "Three miles away up in the hills. We tried to reach it, but they killed many of us before we even got close."

After Banju looked over to Stonner to see if he approved, he said, "We will help you; we will go to their camp and free the captives."

"We may even be able to scare them away for good," Stonner added.

Toreh chuckled. "They all say that, but none of 'em ever return."

"Well," Stonner said as they began to leave, "as we said, we're *different*."

Banju immediately walked out of the tavern and headed back to the camp to get his weapons. "Do you think we should tell Vince about this?"

"Not if we want to proceed with the whole 'save the town' thing," Stonner answered. "He'll give us the whole 'you're too valuable to go off fighting a band of raiders' spiel."

They grabbed their gear and headed toward the hills. They needed to hurry; the storm was getting closer.

The bandits' camp was inside a huge crater by the foothills of a lone mountain. Banju entered it and continued to walk to the center where many of the bandits were entertaining themselves with the card game satarka. They stopped laughing and cheering the winner on when they noticed that Banju was there.

"Good evening, gentlemen." Banju bowed his head. "Fine weather we're having tonight, eh?" Thunder growled in response.

One of the bandits laughed, threw down his cards and began to approach Banju. He was well over three times Banju's size. "Who are you? Nobody walks into our camp and leaves again."

Banju held up a hand. "Now, now, let's not get feisty. I wouldn't step any closer; another step and you die."

The man chuckled and the rest of the bandits in the camp joined in. "Nothing can stop me from reaching you."

"I would not be so sure," Banju replied.

The man spat and took a step. Before his foot even touched the ground he had fallen, an arrow in each leg.

"You see, kind sirs, the day of reckoning has arrived." Banju raised his arms and pointed to two men who had also taken a step; they fell to the ground in agony as an arrow pierced their thighs. "I have come to tell you to leave this town or die."

The bandits parted as a man Banju had burned into his memory stepped to the front, his four-digit hand clasped around a young woman's neck. She seemed to be no older than sixteen. "It is so nice to see you again, boy; we thought that you had died when you fell over the waterfall." He tapped his iron index finger on the girl's neck. She was panting nervously and her blue eyes were open wide with terror. "Lay down your arms or she dies."

Banju wanted to shout and charge at him in anger, but he knew how fruitless that would be.

Instead he said, "Are you such a coward that you would hide behind a woman? I am but one man. Surely you have more faith in your men than that."

The leader clenched his jaw, his auburn eyes revealing nothing. He drew a knife with his left hand and lightly began to trace along the girl's neck. She was whimpering now, tears dripping onto the man's metal finger. "You have a fair point, boy. I don't need to hide behind anyone." He smiled maliciously and slit the woman's throat.

Enraged, Banju roared and charged at the bandits. Arrows took some out before he even reached them. Banju struck mercilessly, striking in a circular pattern. No one was a match for his brutal and quick attacks. He parried one man's thrust and struck another man down. Moving too fast to contemplate his actions, Banju twirled Crikkon to disarm some of the men and sliced open their arms and legs. The group of men continued to get smaller as more fell to his and Stonner's attacks while others retreated in fear. Banju saw the man with the metal index finger running away. *You're not going to escape me so easily,* he thought as he sprinted in pursuit.

The man fell as an arrow lodged itself in his left calf. *Thanks, Stonner.* Banju caught up to the man and hit him in the jaw. "You demon!" He punched him again. "She had a life, a future, and you took it away from her!" He struck the man thrice more. "Tell me: what did you do with my friend?" Banju asked, his voice transformed into a monstrous growl.

Despite the blood flowing out of his mouth, the man chuckled. "He put up a good price on the market; I hear his master fed him to his dogs to see if he would survive. He didn't." He laughed again.

Banju was so infuriated that he raised Crikkon to kill him, but thought better of it at the last second and knocked the man unconscious with its hilt. He returned to the camp and found it deserted save for the bodies of the slain. Despite their sword and arrow wounds, the five bandits had been trampled to death when their compatriots had rushed to escape on horseback.

"Banju," Stonner appeared from behind one of the tents. "I freed the captives and pushed out the rest of the bandits."

Banju collapsed to his knees and stared at the bodies, his blood-covered hands shaking. "What have I done, Stonner? What have I become?"

"Nothing more or less than you were before," Stonner replied softly. "Your blood was hot from the travesty that they performed. Mine was as well; you are not the only one who spilled blood tonight. Come on, we should return soon."

Banju stood but did not move. "We should bury them and bring the girl to her family."

They put the brigands in the pit where the villagers had been kept, filled it with a nearby pile of dirt and rocks and headed back for the village, the young woman's body wrapped in a sack and carried between them.

"Thank you for stopping their leader," Banju said, trying to overcome the dark feelings within him. *I almost killed him…*

Stonner seemed confused. "How do you mean? I never had a clear shot at him."

"Ah, never mind, then." Now Banju was confused; if Stonner had not shot the leader, who had? They had been sure to do the mission alone so as to not compromise anyone else. *And look where that got us.*

Vince greeted them when they returned. "Nice work once again, you two."

"This girl died because of me," Banju pointed out as a squad of knights gingerly took the corpse from them.

"No," Vince replied. "The raiders killed her. And the rest of the villagers got their lives and families back, something that would not have been possible if you two had not intervened. However, you best not go in alone again; next time you may not return."

Stonner sighed and looked up as the first heavy raindrops fell from the stormy clouds. "Just in time, too; the storm is finally here."

Out to Sea

They left the village the next day. The rest of the trip was uneventful; they rode through valley after valley with no more ruins or villages between them and their destination. They were near the outskirts of the harbor's town when Stonner steered his horse close to Banju's and murmured, "We're being watched." Banju glanced behind him and saw Velberk glaring at them. "He's been looking at us for the last half hour or so."

"I take it he still hasn't forgiven us for his brother's defeat," Banju remarked. "We should be careful when we get to Makir; I have a feeling that he may try something."

Stonner nodded and gripped his sword hilt. "Well we'll be ready for him. As far as we know, he's alone in his schemes."

"We should still be careful, though," Banju insisted. "Even if we think he's just a little problem, he might surprise us and give us a run for our gold."

"Oh, most definitely," Stonner replied, though Banju was unsure whether he was being sarcastic or serious.

At that moment their conversation was cut short when Captain Pikt trotted up beside them. "Is something wrong?"

"No, nothing's wrong," Stonner answered.

"Good." Pikt stroked the mane of his horse. "I'd like to congratulate you two on becoming captains in a very short period of time. Now it seems that you and I are family. If you ever need my help, if you need advice or if one of your men disobeys you, let me know. I'll take care of 'em."

"Thank you, Captain," Banju said. "But I don't think that will be necessary."

"Oh but I insist," Pikt said. "You're going to need some respect and protection when we get out on the battlefield, and I can give it to you."

"Thank you, we'll remember that," Banju replied.

Captain Pikt left and Stonner let out a sigh of relief. "I thought he'd never leave! I don't know what it is, but whenever I'm around him a sense of discomfort comes over me."

"Me too."

They arrived at the harbor late that afternoon where hundreds were waiting to watch them embark.

"If you'll excuse me," Vince said to Banju and Stonner as he brushed past them.

Banju and Stonner watched Vince ride over to a young woman. They respectably looked away when the prince dismounted and kissed her. He hugged her, said a few words, kissed her again and jumped back onto his horse.

"Getting a little comfortable with the maids, eh sir?" Stonner commented once he returned.

"Ah, you saw that?" Vince blushed.

Banju shot a warning glance at Stonner, who replied, "It was hard not to, sir. I apologize for invading your privacy."

"It's quite alright, Stonner. Her name's Amelia; I recently proposed to her."

"Well congratulations, sir!" Stonner exclaimed. "You two must be very happy!"

"Yes," Vince replied with a hint of regret in his voice—regret of leaving the one he loved. "We are."

Captain Pikt returned, once again interrupting their chances of talking further. "Are you ready to leave, prince?"

"I am," Vince answered. "Let me give Captains Banju and Stonner some final orders and then I will meet you aboard the *Majestic*."

Pikt bowed his head. "As you wish, sire." He left them in peace.

"Stonner, you will accompany Captain Malco aboard his ship *Adventurer*. Banju, you will accompany General Valerin aboard his ship *Grandeur*.

"Yes, sir." Banju bade farewell to Stonner and left to find the *Grandeur*. He had no success for quite some time; there were dozens of ships preparing to leave that day, and thousands of people were between him and the ship he needed to locate. He finally asked someone for directions and shortly found the ship. It was very huge in Banju's opinion: five hundred feet long, two hundred feet wide and it had six levels beneath the deck. It was a wonder to him that it could even stay afloat.

One of the sailors carrying a small barrel onto the ship bumped into Banju. "Watch where you're goin', boy!"

Banju shook his head and continued his search for the captain's quarters and General Valerin, a task that was much harder than it sounded. He knocked on the door to the quarters but was instead greeted by the first mate.

"What can I do for you, lad?" the first mate asked.

"I am looking for General Valerin," Banju replied. "Do you know where he is?"

"Nay, but if I had to guess I would say that 'e's up in the crow's nest or down in the cargo bay. Do you need help with anythin'?"

"No, not at the moment. Thank you for your time."

"Anytime, mate." The announcement came that they were raising anchor and heading out to sea. "Well, I'd better get on deck now. See you around, lad."

Banju pushed his way on the crowded deck to the portside of the ship so that he could watch the harbor slowly vanish on the horizon and see the dozens of other ships set sail. The sun was setting by the time that Shallor was just a long green line behind them and it was not long before all of the ships vanished, as well, save for the *Grandeur*'s companion, *Daystar*.

With the soothing sea breeze blowing across his face, Banju had time to realize that he had not thought about his father for a few months now. At first he felt ashamed, but then he remembered something that his father had told him years before:

"Soon after your mother died, son, I fell into a great state of depression. However, to my surprise and horror, your mother eventually no longer visited me in my thoughts or dreams. This made me angry with myself, but then I realized something: I had not forgotten her, but had accepted her death and moved on. Now, she visits me like she used to, but it is different than before: I feel happy *when I think of her, not grieved. If and when I die, I would like you to remember me—to honor me—but if you forget me, do not feel as if you have failed me. If you forget me, do not worry; it is only acceptance, and acceptance will lead you to eventual peace of mind and heart. I know that if this happens you will soon remember me again.*

"All I ask is that you remember all of the things that I have taught you and never let anyone tell you what you should believe in; just follow your heart. I'm sure that you will have the strength to get through any obstacle."

Thanks, father, Banju thought. He also remembered the last thing his father had said before his death:

"Things may seem hopeless now, but all you need do is find bird's resting place."

He still did not have the slightest idea what it meant, but he was going to devote a part of his life to finding the "bird's resting place."

The boat lurched on a passing wave and a few of the men's faces turned green and they vomited over the side. Many of the sailors chuckled at this and said that this would probably not be the last time that it would happen. Banju resumed his muses.

Darkness threatened to overcome him as he thought about the girl who had been slain. Selyse had been her name. When her body had been returned to her family, they had broken into sobs. He would never forget the sound of their wails, nor the sight of Selyse's life force spurting out of her neck. *Some of her blood landed on me,* Banju remembered. *I must never forget that. I must be smarter next time, and faster. When we go into battle, no one will die because of me.* He knew that it was wrong, but he buried these feelings and moved on to other thoughts.

Banju wondered how Rik was doing; and, for that matter, if he was still alive. His brother had never sent a message to inform Banju where he had settled and if he was alright or not. He could only hope that Rik had made it safely to his destination and was lucky enough not to run into the group of bandits that Banju and Terin had encountered.

Banju nearly hit himself; it had been a long time since he had thought about Terin, too. He wondered what sort of fate the bandits had given him. The bandit leader had said that he was dead, but who ever trusts the word of a monster? Was he a slave now? Was he dead? Banju feared that the latter was more probable, though the former was just as terrible to consider.

"Hey, kid, you all right?" an elderly sailor asked him.

Banju slightly shook his head to bring his attention back to the here and now. "Oh yeah, I'm fine; I'm just thinking."

The sailor nodded understandingly. "Aye, I've spent many a day watchin' the waves an' thinkin' for hours. The sea offers a clarity that you can't find anywhere else. It's one of the reasons that I joined the Shield Fleet."

"Yes, the sea seems to have that effect on me, too," Banju agreed.

"Well, I best be goin' now; I have a lot to do before we reach Makir. I hope the sea can give you peace as it has given me." The sailor bowed his head in closing and strolled away.

Banju watched the waves for a couple more hours before he decided to go to his cabin and rest. He found it strange that he had been given a cabin that only he slept in; nearly everyone else had to share their cabins with other knights and sailors. *It must come from Vince assigning me as second in command.* The rocking of the ship and exhaustion from his journey helped him drift to sleep faster than he had anticipated.

"The boy is a threat to us," someone was saying, "we can't just let him roam around freely! He might discover his heritage and realize that he can destroy us, just as has happened time and time again!"

"Calm down, my friend," another man, one with a calm and cool voice, said. "It is nigh impossible that he will find out the truth. Besides, I sent my two best assassins out to kill him and his father not too long ago."

"I am aware of this, but your assassin failed! The boy was not present when your assassin reached the village!"

"A minor setback," the calm man insisted.

"Now the boy is a knight and is heading to Makir! Do you know what this means? It means that Makir will fall!"

The calm man raised a hand. "And so be it; our relations with Makir are becoming hostile." He rose from a now visible throne and walked down alongside a large table to where the other man was sitting. "Let's let the boy have his fun. Let's let him become a hero, become overconfident, and then we'll kill him. It will make his death even more enjoyable."

"What if he becomes too strong? What if he becomes one of them?"

The calm man chuckled. "They have been dead for over two centuries now. They will not return."

"Even so, I don't like the fact that we're going to just let him thrive unchallenged."

"Just remind yourself, my friend, that I am in charge here, not you."

202

"I'm beginning to think that you've been in charge for far too long."

"If that's what you really think of me, then so be it." The calm man took a knife from the table and threw it into the other man's right eye, killing him instantly. The "calm" man turned to reveal the left side of his face, of which a terrible scar ran down the entire length. "Does anybody else object to my decision?" Scores of men suddenly appeared in all of the previously vacant seats around the table.

"No, sir!" they all said in unison.

The leader smiled. "Good."

Banju woke up when the ship lurched abruptly. He thought at first that they had hit something, but then he felt the ship resume its journey. He then wondered what had just happened in his dream. This dream had had the same person in it that had been in all of Banju's other previous dreams. *Who is the man with the scar? More importantly, is he a figment of my imagination, or a real human being?* He decided to choose the former, since the latter seemed highly improbable.

He put on a clean shirt and his boots and chose to explore the cargo bay to distract his mind. When he first entered, it was dark, stuffy and foul smelling. He lit a lantern and took it with him into the further bowels of the ship. The cargo bay was filled to the ceiling with wooden crates most likely full of weapons, armor and the like. Banju walked through a

203

small path between them, reminiscent to the maze that he had had to complete during the Five Trials.

There was a ruckus up ahead, and Banju cautiously headed toward the origin of the noise, unsure what he would find down here. "Hello? Anyone there?" He entered another section of the bay that had a bit more space to move around in. A box fell to his left and he shined the lantern over in that direction. "Hello?" He saw a shadow quickly move across the wall. "I see you."

"Be quiet before somebody hears!" a beautiful female voice exclaimed from behind the boxes.

"What are you doing down here?"

She sighed. "What d'you think I'm doing down here? Women aren't allowed on ships or to be in war; we're considered bad luck! This is the only place on this ship that I knew no one would go. That is, until you came along!"

Her impudence shocked and hit him like a barrage of flying arrows. None of the women back in Smith Village ever acted like this. However, there was something familiar about this voice… "Well I for one disagree with those presumptions. Do you have a name?"

When she walked into the light, he nearly dropped the lantern. It was Felicia! She seemed just as surprised to see him as he was her. "Banju? My, of all the people I could've run into down here!" She ran forward and hugged him and then released her hold just enough to look into his eyes, their noses just inches apart. "And what, pray tell, are *you* doing down here?"

"I had a bad dream, so I decided to come down here to stay distracted." He mentally kicked himself. *Why did I just say that?*

Felicia looked at him with a critical eye. "So you came down into a dark, dank, closed space to forget about your dark dreams? This isn't the first place I would have gone."

"Well, you might if this were the only place you haven't yet explored on the entire ship," he pointed out with a shrug.

She bobbed her head. "True."

"So why are you here?" He laughed. "I feel like we already had this conversation back at the banquet."

She smiled, but waved it off. "I am just as good a fighter as any man, so why not? My life is boring, Banju, and it needs some excitement in it before I grow too old to enjoy it." She sat down heavily on one of the crates and sighed. "Besides, my father is on this ship, so someone needs to watch out for him. The gods know he isn't fit for this fight. All my life he has been training me in the arts of the sword and telling me stories about the noble heroes of old. I need to keep him alive. Surely you can understand that…But why am I explaining myself to you? You probably think I'm just a crazy girl who needs to go back home."

Banju gently sat on the crate next to hers. "No, I don't think that. You're defending your family even if it means your death; a noble cause by anyone's standards."

She gazed into his eyes again, her tone softening. "You really think so?"

"I do."

They stared at each other for what felt like several minutes, neither of them uttering a word; Banju felt as if they were exchanging emotions instead. His heart raced and he longed to reach out and embrace her again, or go even further and kiss her. *Would that be wrong? Would I just be acting like a child and letting my impulses get the better of me?* He decided to refrain from letting these thoughts rule him and continued to study her deep, beautiful eyes.

Finally, she broke the silence. "Well, it was nice seeing you again, Banju, but you've most likely got better things to do than stay down here with me all day. If you want to talk again, though, I will be on the second deck tonight. I hear that no one goes there at night."

Banju did not want to leave, but forced himself to say, "I'll see you tonight, then."

With that, she nodded happily in affirmation and disappeared behind the crates again. Banju sighed and went back onto the top deck.

Under the Moonlit Sky

When he reached the deck, he was stopped by one of his fellow knights "Hey you! Can you go up to the galley and inform the cook that the men are restlessly waiting for their supper? Also, see if you can find General Valerin. Thanks!" The knight ran off.

Well that was very polite, Banju remarked to himself. He walked up the stairs to the galley and stopped when he saw a knight clad in full body armor standing in front of the door. "It would be a little uncomfortable, I would think, to stand in full body armor for an entire day," Banju commented.

The knight raised his visor to reveal a shaggy brown beard. "Aye, 'tis not very comfortable, 'specially with sea spray and the sun beatin' down on me at all times. Luckily, I get off at suppertime. Are you here to see the cook?"

"I am, good man."

The knight stepped to the side to give Banju entrance. "Excellent! Could you please tell the cook to speed up his cooking for my sake? Tell him that I, Sir Gregor, am hungry."

"I will do my best, sir."

"Thank you kindly!"

Banju walked into the galley and took a moment to breathe in all of the appetizing aromas of the fresh vegetables, fruits, meats, spices and breads. The smell reminded him that he had not had anything to eat for quite some time. Ladles, pots, pans, carrots, onions, tomatoes, apples, berries, salt, pepper and other spices hung on the walls.

A short and stubby man stood over a boiling pot. He was anxiously cutting up vegetables, putting them in the pot and stirring. A tall and muscular man entered from the storage area, picked up a ladle and took a sip of the cook's concoction.

"Needs more salt," the tall man advised.

"I've already put enough salt in it," the cook objected. "If I put in anymore, we'll have enough to turn a freshwater lake into a saltwater one! I say it's finished."

The tall man glared down at the shorter man. "Who's in charge here? You or me?"

The cook looked remorsefully down at the floor. "You, General Valerin, but…"

"Salt," the tall man said roughly, "needs more salt. End of story."

"Excuse me." Both of them turned to look at Banju, frustration clearly visible on their faces. "I was sent to tell the cook that Sir Gregor is hungry, along with everyone else on board."

Valerin looked down at the cook reprovingly. "You heard him, Cook. Go give Sir Gregor some food and then take over his watch."

The chef took his hat off and held his hands in a praying gesture. "P-please let me stay! S-somebody has to make the supper!"

"I'll cook the food tonight," Valerin announced. "I'm a much better cook, anyhow."

"B-b-but…but I—"

"Get out now! Get out before I throw you out!"

As the cook scrambled to get out of the galley, Banju stepped closer to Valerin. The General sighed. "That cook has been on my nerves since we started this voyage. I don't know why King Banton assigned him to my ship; it must have been so that he could get a good laugh. Boy am I going to give that king an earful when we get back!"

Banju smiled politely. "Is there anything I can help you with?"

"Hand me that salt over there." Valerin opened one of the windows, picked up the cook's pot and dumped it over the side. He then grabbed a new pot, filled it with water and set it on the cooking fire. "Other than that, just wait for further instructions."

Banju put the salt on a counter near the pot. "Yes, sir."

When the water boiled, Valerin poured in noodles. "What's your name, son?"

"Banju, sir."

"It is very nice to meet you, Banju. My name is Valerin, but I bet that you already knew that. Could you hand me that celery over there? No, not that one, the one to your right; that's it." Valerin grabbed a knife, threw the celery up into the air above the pot and cut it into small pieces before gravity pulled it into the pot.

Impressed, Banju asked, "How long did it take you to learn that?"

Valerin shrugged. "I can't remember, but it was quite a few years back." He wiped sweat off of his brow and said, "We're lucky we're not feeding the entire crew, otherwise this would take a lot longer." Seeing the confused look on Banju's face, he explained, "Only a quarter of the crew actually comes to supper. The rest of the crew have their own supply of food, thus they stay in their cabins and eat their own meals. I may be making three pots of food tonight, but if the entire troop came down for supper, three pots wouldn't be nearly enough."

The General stirred the pot and heaved a big sigh of relief. "Now that it's finished, I really need your help. I need you to take this pot down to the mess hall nearest to the knights' quarters. You can stay there and eat with the crew if you wish, or you can come and eat with me and my men." He handed the heavy pot to Banju. "Watch your step; make sure you don't trip. Thank you for doing this, Captain."

Banju followed his instructions and gingerly brought the enormous pot down to the mess hall. As he entered the hall he heard an elderly sailor talking to a circle of knights in a corner of the room.

"Oh aye," the sailor was saying, "'Tis a fearsome beast, so it is."

"You're absurd," one of the knights objected. "I think that the years you have spent on the sea have finally made you crazy; there is no such thing as the beast you speak of."

The sailor raised a slightly trembling finger. "But I have seen the remains of ships that have been attacked with my own two eyes!"

"Our discussion is done, crazy old man!"

"Fellow knight, are you just going to stand there all day with the food?" another knight asked Banju.

Banju set the pot on the middle of the center table. "No, of course not."

"Supper is here!" When someone shouted this, everyone rushed to find a seat, and Banju smoothly managed to sit by the sailor he had heard speaking when he had first entered the hall.

Once they filled their bowls, Banju whispered to the old man, "What is this fearsome beast I heard you mention?"

The sailor's rough white beard seemed to crack when he smiled. "I'm glad that you took an interest in my story. Us sailors know it to be a real beast that lurks these waters, while others—like your friends over there—believe it to be only a myth. It is called the Kry'vogh."

Banju shuddered. He had heard a few stories about it, none of which he remembered to be pleasant. "The Kry'vogh has been around for hundreds of years," the sailor continued. He took a bite of his supper. "Mmm, delicious. Nobody quite knows where its origins lie, but many of us believe that it evolved from a *very* giant squid." He chuckled. "Huh, 'course, nobody's ever been able to find out what it really looks like, 'cause whoever has encountered it is dead!"

"How big is it?"

The sailor coughed quietly to clear his throat. "No one knows for sure, but it's at least big enough to take a huge ship like this 'un down to the depths."

Banju's food tasted like ash in his mouth as he listened.

"It can live on fish alone, but it prefers human flesh above all."

"And where does it usually strike?"

"Many believe that it strikes in random patterns, but based upon the wreckage we've found I have discovered that the Kry'vogh has a 'strike zone.' If anyone enters it, the Kry'vogh will attack them. Why, as luck would have it, we're going to be passing near it!"

"Cliver, don't scare the kid with your ridiculous stories!" a knight exclaimed.

Cliver stood up. "You'd best believe in me stories, mate! I'll tell ye what, let's make a bet: If this ship is still floating by the end of this voyage, you've won and I owe you twenty gold coins; but if it's sunk, I've won and you've, well, died."

The knight smiled, sure that he would win. "It's a deal!"

"This is the easiest bet I've ever made," Cliver remarked as he sat back down.

"You really think we're going to be attacked?" Banju asked him.

Cliver shook his head. "I don't think so, I know so. I was quite pleased when I signed up for this ship to learn that I would have the honor of meeting the Kry'vogh face to face. It is best to be prepared and know where you're going in the afterlife, mate. Luckily, I know that my daughter will be back home on solid ground if this ship sinks."

"Your daughter?"

"Aye, my daughter, Felicia." He chuckled. "Silly girl wanted to come along, but I told her that she had to stay with her aunt!"

Banju kept on eating, trying to conceal his surprise. "Why would she want to come along?"

"She's got her mother's fighting spirit; once she has an objective, nothing can stop her 'cept death itself! Now that I think about it, I regret not allowing her to come; she would've been a valuable asset to this crew an' the army." He shrugged. "Oh well. Can't change anything now, I s'pose. And it's for the best, in any case."

Banju nodded, finished his stew and excused himself. "I really should be going, Cliver. It was nice meeting you."

Cliver waved and slurped his stew before it could escape his spoon. "Aye, likewise. See you tomorrow, my new friend!"

Banju left the mess and went up to the second deck: a small deck near the bow of the ship that was elevated above the bigger main deck by four thick wooden beams. An odd place for a deck, to be sure, but Banju was pleased to find that it was deserted just as Felicia had presumed. He sat on a coil of huge, thick rope and watched the sun sink over the horizon. Before long his thoughts began to drift. *If we survive this voyage, am I going to survive the upcoming battle? King Banton seems to think that we stand a chance, but since Sarkk has the Golden Gauntlet, that slims our chances to little to none. If only we had a Gauntlet, too; or maybe a Drifter of old.*

He looked up at the first star to appear in the sky. *Creator, if you can hear me, please protect us from Sarkk's evil forces and help us purge the lands of people like him. I know I'm making this sound like a small and easy request—and to you, it might be; but without your assistance and guidance this could all just be a hopeless endeavor.* Banju bowed his head and let his emotions finally be released from the confines of his mind, a teardrop sliding down his left cheek. *And, Lord, give me strength to fight through my first battle and forgive me for any lives I may take.*

The celestial light twinkled in response, soon followed by the twinkling of the stars around it. Banju smiled and no longer felt alone, knowing the Creator of All was watching over him.

"Gazing at the stars, Banju?" someone asked.

Banju twirled around and saw that Felicia was sitting on one of the wide railings, her back resting against one of the supports of the foremast and her arms wrapped around her knees to hold them close to her chest. "No," he replied, "I was praying."

214

"A pretty emotional prayer, by the look of it," she gestured at the tear on his cheek.

He rubbed his cheek and his eyes to ensure that no more were threatening to fall. "Yes, well, it's been a while since I've done it."

She nodded understandingly.

Eager to change the subject after being caught vulnerable, he said, "I met your father today at supper."

Felicia gazed at him intensely as if expecting him to say something detestable next. "And?"

"And he seemed pleased to announce that you are back home while he is out here about to get eaten by the Kry'vogh."

She laughed. "Then I'm guessing he told you his stories?" He nodded. "He always loves to tell those stories whenever he has the chance. Do you believe him?"

"Do you?"

She shrugged and gracefully stepped onto the deck and stood by the bow, looking over the rail and down into the water. "The wrecks he's found support his claims, but a part of me still refuses to believe that there could be such a beast out there."

Banju leaned next to her. "It *does* seem rather unlikely."

"But if it's true..." Her voice cut off and she resumed gazing into his eyes, affection showing clearly in hers. "If you knew you were going to die and you couldn't escape it, where would you want to be?"

Letting his impulses control him this time, Banju gently held her hands in his. "I would want to be here, with you, under the moonlit sky."

"If what you say is true, and if we are really going to die within the next few days," she put her face closer to his, her voice growing tender, "then I won't have to regret this." She kissed him squarely on the lips: a kiss like none that Banju could have ever imagined. They could feel their mutual love flow through them as it was exchanged through the kiss. Neither one wanted it to end; they stood locked for what seemed like a lifetime.

It was finally broken when the ship rocked from a wave.

Felicia smiled, and Banju smiled back. "Banju, I know that we have only known each other for a short time, and this may sound ridiculous…but I love you; more than I've ever loved anyone else."

Is this really happening? he thought. Never had he thought it possible for two individuals to fall so far in love so quickly. "I love you, too," he said.

They stood there, clasped in each other's arms and staring at the moon as it reflected off of the water until sleep called them to depart.

"I will see you tomorrow, Banju, my love." She left him with a gentle kiss.

Dinner with the General

Banju woke the next morning refreshed and oddly at peace. He walked up to the deck with a kick in his step, laid down on a pile of coiled rope on the deck he had talked with Felicia on and dreamily looked up at the blowing sail and the blue sky above as he munched on a block of granola he had found in his food satchel. Of all the nights and things he had experienced over the years, none could match the previous night. Had it really happened? Could it have been a dream? He pinched himself to make sure.

So this is what love feels like, he thought with relish. He could have contentedly spent the rest of the day lying on that pile of rope, but alas, a knight found him around noon.

"Captain Banju, sir?" the knight asked.

"Aye," he responded. "Do you need me for something?"

The knight did not reply immediately, forming his words carefully. He appeared to be no older than Banju and seemed to be taking no chances of losing his newly acquired position. "No, sir, not me, but General Valerin requested that I inform you that he would like you to dine with him tonight instead of the crew. He did not tell me anything else."

Banju quietly sighed and put his hands behind his head. He had been hoping to spend the evening with Felicia. "Very well. Thank you for informing me."

The messenger bowed his head. "Of course, Captain."

As the knight walked away, Banju undesirably stood up. If he could not spend dinner with Felicia, then he would spend lunch with her instead. He stopped in the mess hall, grabbed a tray of food being served and headed for the lower decks.

"Banju, I wanted to apologize for last night," Felicia said after she took a bite of the bread and turkey that he had brought her.

"Apologize for what?"

"I…I fear that I acted out of line." She blushed slightly. "I let my impulses control my actions and—"

"You have nothing to be ashamed of," he squeezed her hand reassuringly, "in fact, I acted out of impulse, too. But that doesn't matter; what matters is whether or not we spoke from our hearts last night. Did you?"

She contemplated it for a moment and then nodded. "Yes, I believe I did."

"Then there is nothing to regret."

"Thanks, Banju." She smiled and kissed him on the cheek.

"On a different note," Banju said, "how do you plan to join in the coming battle?"

Felicia beamed. "I am going to dress like a knight; in the fray, no one will notice anything strange about me."

"And the thought that you should stay and guard the ship never crossed your mind?"

"I came to fight, Banju, not to twiddle my thumbs and anxiously await your return."

They spent the rest of their meal in silence. Once they finished eating, Banju regrettably explained to Felicia that he needed to return to the top deck before his dinner with General Valerin. She leaned over and kissed him softly on the lips. "But I will see you here tomorrow, won't I?"

"I wouldn't miss it in a thousand years," Banju said as he turned to leave.

To Banju's relief, nothing eventful happened between then and dinner, giving him time to ponder why the General wanted to talk to him. *Did I do something wrong?* The General had mentioned the day before that Banju could dine with him, so this theory seemed highly unlikely. Whatever the reason, he was about to find out.

He knocked on the General's door and waited with trepidation.

"Come in; the door's unlocked," came a reply from inside.

Banju pushed the door open and saw that the room was empty save for two officers and General Valerin sitting at a table with hands clasped. Directly behind him was an enormous window that went from floor-to-ceiling and wall-to-wall and overlooked the calm ocean and the setting sun. Trophies and weapons lined the wall to his left, and a huge, detailed map of Shallor, the ocean and Makir covered the desk to his right.

"Please, Sir Banju, take a seat," Valerin gestured to the chair across from his own. As Banju sat, Valerin said, "This is Sir Mared," a red-bearded man to Valerin's left bowed his head, "and this is Lieutenant Trey." The other man nodded and gave Banju a weary look. "We were just discussing our battle plans," Valerin said. "Lieutenant, if you please."

Trey cleared his throat and repositioned himself in his chair. "King Banton has given us and the *Daystar* the order to attack Makir from the south. There is a bay that goes miles inland, and it is from there that I propose we land."

"Do you think that Sarkk will have a fleet there?" Sir Mared inquired.

"It is likely," Valerin said. "He is planning to attack us, after all."

"So how are we going to reach the bay?"

Trey poured himself some wine before replying, "If we arrive at nightfall, their guard will not be sufficient enough to hold us back. All we must do is sink Sarkk's ships, and then the bay is ours."

Valerin nodded. "I think that this is a possibility. Sarkk's forces will be spread thin by then, making our job much simpler. Will you two be joining us for dinner?"

Sir Mared sighed. "Would that I could; I must check our inventory to ensure that we can perform this operation."

"And I must share this plan with our other squad leaders," Lieutenant Trey added.

"Very well. I will see you two on the morrow." Once Trey and Mared had left, Valerin asked Banju, "I trust the crew has been working diligently these past couple of days?"

"To my knowledge, sir."

"Good." Valerin relaxed and leaned back in his seat. "I'm sure you've been wondering why I called you here tonight." He smiled at this. "And don't worry; you're not in any kind of trouble. I simply wanted to get to know my second in command better and understand why the prince has put so much trust in you."

"To tell you the truth, General, I've been wondering the same thing. I asked him about it once, but he didn't give me a direct response."

"Perhaps it is because of his childhood." Banju raised his eyebrows in inquiry, expecting him to mention Peter's death, and Valerin continued, "You see, being a prince may sound like a dream come true for anyone, but it has its drawbacks. When he was a child, he had no real friends—only those who pretended to be because of his wealth and name. You and Stonner are the closest things that he has to actual friends."

Banju contemplated these words, thinking back to the other traumatizing childhood event that Vince had shared with him. "He never mentioned anything like that to us."

"He wouldn't; pride prevents him from admitting such a thing." There was a knock on the door. "Ah, that would be our dinner!"

The chef that Valerin had kicked out of the galley the day before warily walked in carrying two trays of food. "H-here's your steaks, sir." He set them down on the table.

"Thank you," Valerin said, "that will be all."

The chef bowed. "Of course, sir." With that, he hastily left the room.

"Now enough about the prince," Valerin said as he cut into his steak, "I want to hear about you."

"I'm afraid there's not much to tell, sir."

Valerin looked at Banju with compassion and understanding, completely obliterating Banju's previous fears. "Enlighten me."

"Well, my mother died before I was old enough to remember her. I have spent my life working alongside my father as a blacksmith at the Arrow's Hammer in Smith Village. Perhaps you've heard of it?" Valerin nodded. "If fate had not played a cruel trick on me, I would have lived out the rest of my days there. But as it were, my father was murdered less than a year ago for reasons unknown." He shrugged and took a bite. "So here I am, living out the only dream that I have left."

Silence then filled the room, the only sounds being that of their forks and knives against their plates. Valerin seemed to see right through him.

"You are a very interesting man, Banju. The wild card of the Royal Army, if you will."

"How so?"

"Many men join the Royal Army in hopes of fame or fortune…But not you. Others are driven by their lust for battle…But not you. Still others enlist to fight for land-wide peace and Shallor." He looked Banju square in the eyes. "But not you."

"I don't know what you mean, sir."

Valerin set his fork and knife down. "What is it that drives you? Is it revenge for your father's murder, or is it hope that you will become so occupied fighting for the king that you will forget your personal tragedies? You certainly aren't doing it to fulfill a 'life-long dream.'" Banju began to feel uncomfortable and wondered where he was going with this. "Currently, this army is full of men who do not know the reason that they fight and die. In the coming battle, these men need to know what they are fighting for, and why. And what are they fighting for? Peace. Security. Family. Death will come to hundreds, maybe thousands, of our troops, but if they die for a cause they will die in peace." He leaned forward in his chair. "I'm prepared to die for peace, Banju. Are you?"

His appetite gone, Banju excused himself, returned to his quarters and fell asleep deeply troubled. What *was* he willing to die for?

His fitful sleep was cut short when a storm brewed around the ship, making it toss and turn from the wind and waves. At first he tried to fall back asleep, but then he began to worry about Felicia all alone in the bowels of the ship. He shuddered at the thought of loose crates falling upon her and decided that he would go down and make sure that she was all right.

Grabbing a lantern, he headed for the stairs, a difficult task in the violently rocking ship.

"Felicia," he called once he reached the cargo bay. "Felicia, it's me, Banju."

She appeared out of the shadows and wrapped her arms around him. "My knight has come to save me from this dreadful storm! Tell me, Sir Knight, what is your plan?"

"Come with me to my quarters; you'll be safer there than you are here."

"But won't someone see me?"

"They're all too busy worrying about the storm. Come on, follow me." He took her back to his quarters, and just as he had predicted, no one seemed to notice them. "There, you see? We made it!" He smoothed out the blanket on his bed. "Alright…you sleep here, and I'll sleep by the door."

She sat on the bed and smiled at him flirtatiously. "You know, there's room enough on this bed for two."

Unfazed, Banju said, "Yes, but if I sleep by the door, no one will be able to barge in here and discover that this ship has a stowaway." As an afterthought, he added, "Besides, I don't think I'm ready for that."

She smiled at him again—this time as if he had passed some sort of test—then took off her boots and lay back on the bed. "Look at that; he's good-looking *and* wise. Until morning, my love."

"Goodnight, Felicia." He blew out the lantern and took up his position by the door. Despite the fact that it was uncomfortable, he slept better there than he had in his bed only hours before.

The Kry'vogh

"Banju, Banju, wake up!"

He opened his eyes and saw that Felicia was standing right above him. "What is it?"

"There's someone at the door." As if on cue, the door shook from a steady knock on the other side.

"Okay, hide behind the bed while I see who it is." She complied, and he opened the door.

"Oh, thank the Creator!" It was Cliver, and he seemed to be slightly frightened. "I've been trying to get to you for a long time."

"Sorry; I must have been out cold. What's the matter, Cliver?"

"Our watchmen spotted a strange bird following us last night during the storm." There was a hint of fear in Cliver's voice. "General Valerin says it's a dragon."

"A dragon?"

"That's not the least of our worries, mate," he said, "the storm took us off course; we're still going toward Makir, but we've lost sight of the *Daystar*. And there's something else…you'd better get on deck right away."

"Why?"

"While I was on deck, I saw sharks fleeing west."

"What does that mean?"

Cliver's voice dropped to a whisper. "The Kry'vogh is coming."

"Have you warned the crew?"

"Aye," Cliver replied in a sad tone. "But they won't listen to me. They think I'm going insane. You best get on deck so you can have the best chance of survival."

"I'll be there in a moment."

"I will wait for you there."

Banju shut the door and began to hastily put on his attire. "Felicia, did you hear that?"

She stood from her hiding place, her face pale. "What do you plan to do?"

He grabbed Crikkon and headed for the door. "Survive. Come with me to the armory; we're going to give this monster a battle to remember."

Once they reached it, Banju put chain mail over his clothes. He had heard stories of warriors avoiding shark bites by wearing chain mail, so perhaps it would protect him from the Kry'vogh, as well. Banju tightened the strap around Crikkon to ensure that he would not lose it in a brawl or under the water. He then grabbed a hatchet, a bow and some arrows. Felicia grabbed a cutlass and put on a lightly armored vest and helm to hide her female physique.

"When we reach the deck, wait a few moments before following me," Banju ordered. "That way your father won't suspect that you're anyone but a typical sailor." They soon found Cliver and Banju gestured to him with the hatchet. "I'm not going down without a fight, what about you?"

"My days are long overdue," Cliver said with a smile slowly spreading across his face. "Don't let it take you, too."

"I won't let you die," Banju promised.

"No, no! Your first priority right now is you and you alone. You still have many years ahead of you, my friend, and the king is going to need you in the upcoming battle. Here," he carefully handed Banju a sheathed dagger. "This is poison-tipped. If you are taken under, stab anything within your reach."

Banju grabbed the hilt. "And what about you?"

Cliver unbuttoned his vest to reveal dozens of knives. "I will put up a good fight."

"Is this really what you want?"

"Aye," Cliver said firmly. "What is a better way to die than to be eaten by a legend, eh?"

"Living," Banju replied.

Cliver laughed at his smart remark. "Aye, mate, you're right." He offered his hand. "It was a pleasure meeting you."

Banju shook it. "The pleasure was all mine."

"Oh, one other thing: Once you get back to Shallor, could you write a poem or story about me? I would hate to get eaten by a legend for nothing!"

Banju smiled. "Very well, I promise that I will put you down in history."

"That's good to know." Cliver smiled one last time before disappearing in the crowd that was ever increasing on the deck.

Felicia stood beside him. "That was most likely the last chance you would've had to speak with your father," Banju said.

"It's better this way; he still thinks I'm back home and safe. Let him die in peace."

Banju was about to comment when he heard words that made his stomach tighten.

"The dragon is approaching!" a sailor shouted from the crow's nest.

"Archers at the ready! Spearmen behind them! Let's give this dragon something to cry about!" Valerin ordered.

"Come on!" Banju led Felicia to the center of the ship, hatchet at the ready. He had a good feeling that the dragon was not the only thing that was going to attack, and by the look on Valerin's face, he seemed to know that, too.

The ship rocked violently, sending many men hurtling over the sides.

"What was that?" asked a knight.

"Did we hit a reef or something?" a sailor asked.

"Nay, mates," Cliver yelled over the racket that the scared men were making, "'tis what I've been trying to tell ye all along: the Kry'vogh is here!"

"That's non—" that man was pulled off the boat by a giant tentacle.

"It's here!" an archer shouted as he shot an arrow at the retreating arm.

Five dark green tentacles—three times taller than the ship and as thick as huge tree trunks—rose from the water on both sides of the ship.

"Shoot them, archers; make 'em look like pincushions!"

The archers fired, but only a few arrows actually made contact, for the tentacles came crashing down on the ship with a force stronger than anyone could have imagined. Where the tentacles landed men were squashed and the deck was crushed to splinters.

Banju winced as he listened to the dying screams of dozens of knights and sailors and watched as others were pulled off the ship and into the water. When he saw one of the huge limbs coming for him and Felicia, he hit it with the axe and stabbed it with an arrow. Blue blood trickled out of the small gashes that he had made, but even with these injuries the tentacle barely slowed its advance. He thought for sure that it was over until a huge man carrying the largest axe Banju had ever seen brought the blade down heavily on the tentacle, slicing it all the way through to the deck.

Banju saluted in thanks and decided that they might stand a better chance if they went up to the crow's nest. Dodging other tentacles and dying men writhing across the ship, they successfully made it. Dozens more men were taken under and other parts of the ship were torn apart by the powerful and fearsome Kry'vogh. The entire stern of the ship was in ruins now, making the bow point to the sky and the ship itself lurch upward at a forty-five degree angle.

Scores of men fell off of the ship; some simply by losing their balance in the sudden angle change and others by being pulled roughly off by the relentless Kry'vogh. Other men, Banju knew, had not been lucky enough to get to the top deck before the attack; many had likely perished in their cabins, in the mess hall or somewhere else in the lower levels of the vessel. Only about a third of the crew had been on deck when the attack began.

The sound of painful wails filled Banju's ears, and it was all that he could do to keep his senses alert and stop his emotions from taking over. He was scared, positive that his life would soon end; Felicia anxiously held his left hand. Banju thought back to all that he had not accomplished; he had not found his father's killer, his knighthood was short-lived and he would never be able to marry Felicia.

He shook his head. *Snap out of it! This is no time for regrets! You're not dead yet!*

Forcing himself to stay focused on survival, he took in the surroundings away from the ship. It would have been a peaceful day had the Kry'vogh not attacked! He almost jumped when he noticed the dragon was still approaching. He grabbed his bow and prepared to fire; but before he could, *more* tentacles popped out of the water, surrounded the dragon and began to drag it down into the water. That was when Banju noticed that there was someone *riding* the dragon. It was too far away for him to see any distinguishable features before it was dragged under, but he was sure that someone had been riding the dragon like a horse.

Further random thoughts were stopped when he heard and felt the mast that they were on begin to crack and bend over the water at almost parallel. Fear and adrenaline shot back into him and he knew that they only had a few precious seconds to make a move or they would perish.

To his dismay, a tentacle shot up and wrapped itself around Felicia's leg. "Banju!" Felicia began to fall before he had a chance to react.

"Felicia!" He barely managed to grab her hand and hold on tightly to what was left of the crow's nest.

"Banju, you need to let go of me!"

Tears began to form in his eyes. "No, Felicia, I won't let you die! I love you!"

She looked into his watery eyes, her gaze piercing through all the panic and fear that he had accumulated. "Banju," she repeated, her voice oddly calm in spite of the situation. "Everything is going to be okay, my love. I want this. Let. Me. Go."

He did so, and pain struck his chest. She gave him a slight smile before being ungracefully enveloped by the ocean with a *snap*. *I…I can save her! There's still hope!* Blinded by grief, he dove in after her.

The impact into the water almost caused Banju to scream in pain. The fact that the water was nearly ice cold amplified these feelings. He tried to swim to the surface but only managed a quick breath before a tentacle grabbed him by the waist and pulled him back under. In only seconds he was two fathoms below the surface, the pressure beginning to form a dizzying feeling within Banju's ears and eyes. He desperately unsheathed the poison-tipped dagger and stab-bed his adversary. A deafening roar erupted around him, augmented by the water. He felt the tentacle's grip loosen slightly, but it still continued to pull him deeper and deeper into the depths.

Visibility was limited, but Banju soon noticed a silvery shiny round object in front of him. It was just about as big as Banju and he suspected that it was a sinking shield. That is, until he noticed that a black dot at the center of it seemed to be staring directly at *him. This must be one of the Kry'vogh's eyes.* With the poison-tipped dagger still in hand, he pushed it as hard as he could right into its center. There was another earsplitting roar, and then the tentacle finally released him.

As he struggled to reach the surface, he took one last look below him. The Kry'vogh was sinking down to the dark depths, the remains of the *Grandeur* and the crew in its arms, including his love, Felicia. Heartbreak, anguish and despair gripped Banju; he was the lone survivor of the attack with no food, supplies or a way to continue his voyage; even if he managed to reach the surface, he was as good as dead. *Is that so bad?*

Giving into his exhaustion and emptiness, Banju sank into unconsciousness as the pressure around him grew unbearable.

Into the Dark Mist

He was walking in the shallows of a misty, dark lake, wearing only ripped, black clothes. He could barely move his legs through the thickness of the water. It seemed more like stone than water, but slowly but surely he was wading to the gray shore. The sky was pitch-black save for a small glint of moonlight escaping through the dark clouds. He knew somehow that this was a place that no man alive had been before. He finally made it to the shore and stopped when he noticed a bearded man approaching. Banju stopped only because he thought that the man looked familiar.

The man seemed confused. "Banju, why are you here?"

Banju was just as confused as he. "I don't know."

"Surely you're not dead? Nay; I did not foresee you dying so soon."

"Wh-who are you?"

The man chuckled and raised his hands in exasperation, revealing a black scar on his right palm. "It's been almost a year, hasn't it? You've changed since the last time I saw you; you're stronger and a lot more confident now than you were back then, but at the same time you have grown weaker…"

His memory was slowly coming back to him now. "You're the man I met the day my brother left!"

The man nodded in confirmation. "Indeed I am, my boy! And now I realize that you're not dead," he flashed Banju a confident smile. "I was wise to give you my gift."

Banju was as confused as ever. "What gift was that?"

The strange man laughed heartily. "The gift that I gave you. I cannot tell you anymore, Banju; it is for you to figure out. I am sorry, but I must go now."

Banju stopped him before he could walk away. "Wait! May I ask you one question?"

"Go ahead, but choose wisely; I will only answer one. The rest you must figure out for yourself."

"What happened to you after you left Smith Village?"

The man's expression saddened slightly. "They found me. It was only a matter of time before they would find me after I left, so I knew my time was coming. That is why I gave you my gift." He turned to walk up into the gloomy dunes. "Farewell, Banju, and fare thee well on your quest. Continue working diligently and you will come out victorious. Oh, and don't touch anyone here; if you do, you will be lost here forever."

"Wait, don't go! Who are they?" The man vanished into thin air, leaving Banju alone on the dark beach.

His loneliness was short lived, however, when he saw a much more familiar figure walking toward him. "Father!"

"It is good to see you again, Banju." His father still had the four gaping wounds on his chest and his expression told Banju that he was in anguish. "However, I wish you weren't here."

"Why? What is this place?"

Thanju stopped him when he tried to get closer. "This is a very bad place, Banju; for you, anyway. It's not always this dark and melancholy. Usually it's a wonderful and joyful place."

Realization finally hit Banju, making his face turn pale. "This is the afterlife, isn't it?"

"In a way it is, my son. This place is more of a meeting place rather than the afterlife. But please, you must go before you're stuck here."

"No, father, I don't want to leave you again!"

"You must," Thanju persisted. "I believe in you, son, and I know for a fact that you will succeed in your quest and in whatever else you decide to do."

"Please, father, don't make me leave!"

"Stay strong, my son." Thanju's voice was almost a whisper now, and his body began to fade. "And whatever you do, don't give up."

"Father, no!"

A seagull yelped nearby. He could feel a gentle breeze blowing across his face and the calm rocking motion of a ship. His mouth was dry, his eyes felt like they were burning and his entire body was aching. There was a sharp pain in his right leg, but other than that he felt like his body would recover in a couple of days. When the ability to smell finally came back to him, he could smell the scent of burning fish and the discernable odor of the sea. There was a loud crash of falling pots, and a man swore.

Banju figured it was time that he opened his eyes. Blue sky was the first thing he saw, and then he turned his head and saw the tossing sea and moved his eyes to where he had heard the noise. He was on a large raft, but other than that, he had no idea where he was.

He almost jumped when a man about his own age appeared right above him. "Ah, you finally woke up! You had me worried there for a second, mate! I wasn't sure if you were having death convulsions or just phantasmagoric dreams!" The young man had wavy dark hair that went just below his ears, cold blue eyes, slightly pale skin and a small red scar above his right dark eyebrow. He wore a black cloak and boots, and a slightly curved sword hung at his side.

Banju tried to ask him who he was, but his mouth was too dry for him to utter anything other than a gargle.

"Oh, where are my manners?" The anomalous young man held a canteen to Banju's lips. "You must be parched after a battle like that!"

After Banju had rehydrated, he asked, "Who are you?"

"This is usually the part where we would exchange our uninteresting back-stories, but I will spare you that by only sharing my name: the name's William." The man closed his canteen. "Though some call me Will, Bill, dog, coward, pirate, cheater, liar and other names not worth mentioning at this time and—"

"My name's Banju," Banju interrupted before the conversation could go *too* far astray.

William looked deep in thought and sat down on a stool by one of the billowing sails. "'Banju,' 'Banju,' where have I heard that name before?" He shrugged dramatically. "No matter, it will come to me later; at least you're alive. I watched the entire brawl from a safe distance away. You were very resourceful, Banju; you're the only person I've seen survive a clash with the Kry'vogh. Myself excluded, of course." He leaned forward. "Now if I may be so bold, may I ask why a huge armada was passing through my friend's—the Kry'vogh's—territory?"

"We were heading for Makir."

William's face grew stern. "Going off to fight Sarkk and his army, eh? Well I assure you, the rest of your fleet made it safely through."

Banju let out a sigh of relief. "Good! Thank you for saving me, William, I owe you one."

"No problem, mate, it's always a pleasure to help someone else."

"Might I ask if there were any other survivors?" he inquired, a hint of hope in his voice.

Will tapped his forehead with a finger, as if jogging it for any lost details. "Nope, I'm afraid not."

Banju bowed his head and tears welled up in his eyes. *Felicia!*

Will sat by him and laid a comforting hand on one of his shoulders.

"I'm sorry, Banju; you must've lost many friends on that ship. But you must realize: there is nothing that you could have done; the Kry'vogh is an inexorable force that cannot be stopped until it has had its fill. It knows no pity." He winked. "Lucky for you, it was satisfied enough to let you escape."

Banju ignored his attempts at comfort at first, but soon began to regrettably accept them. *The only thing I can do now is focus on the task at hand. It'll at least help me keep my mind off of her.* "I know that this is probably asking too much, but is there any way that you can take me to Makir?"

Will chuckled and adjusted the rudder. "Wow, you're real observant! Look around you, my new friend!"

The sky was dark, and a landmass of dark gray mountains could be seen stretching across the entire horizon.

"This is Makir, Banju: A dark place where sunlight only reaches through the thick clouds on the rarest of occasions. Unfortunately, there is only one way to get you there without much of a fuss."

"And how is that?" Banju asked.

Will bowed his head. "Sorry, mate, but you're going to have to go back to sleep."

Banju's head began to spin. *He drugged the water!* he thought before he slipped back into unconsciousness.

Enslaved

"Hey! This one's-a-stirrin'!" a gravelly voice shouted out.

Banju woke—his head pounding—and tried to move, but to no avail.

"He's trying to break out of his bonds!" the same voice exclaimed.

"Shut your yappin' chops," a stronger and deeper voice said, "I'll take care of him."

Banju was lifted by the neckline of his tunic and stared a tall, dark man right in his glaring gray eyes. "You better not try somethin' foolish now; we've been going through slaves like good biscuits 'n' gravy lately, so we need you. Understand?"

Banju nodded, still trying to adjust to these new surroundings.

The huge slaver roughly threw him back on the ground. "Good. Bilk, untie this boy and put him to work."

The smaller man—the one with the gravelly voice—whined, "Now why d'you have to go an' call me 'Bilk' again for, Grud?"

Grud shrugged his huge, muscular shoulders. "It's a nickname. Besides, it suits you well considering you never paid Tunny for that slave you 'bought' in Kiranda and the way you evaded those authorities in Contor."

Bilk pointed a finger at Grud's huge face. "Now listen here: the gods know that I paid Tunny every silver piece for that slave back in Kiranda." He thought for a moment. "But those blasted soldiers in Contor never saw me again, for sure."

Banju sat listening to this odd exchange and tried to figure out exactly where he was. He was inside of a poorly set up tent that had huge fur blankets acting as makeshift walls. There was a cooking station to his right that had many knives, ladles and pots, one of which was boiling over a small fire. To his left were racks of clothes: mostly thick fur cloaks and boots. He slowly and carefully started to slither toward the knives on a cutting board as the two slavers continued to banter.

"However," Grud was saying, "you wouldn't have eluded Sarkk's men if it hadn't been for that cursed blizzard."

Banju stopped for a moment. *A blizzard in Makir?* He looked out of the open entrance for the first time and realized that it was lightly snowing outside. *What's going on here?*

"Yea, what can I say; the gods are on my side!" Bilk said proudly.

Banju grabbed one of the knives, put it in his right boot and lay back where Grud had thrown him.

Grud shook his head. "I grow tired of this conversation. I'm going out to make sure the slaves are working up to my standards."

Once he exited, Bilk approached Banju and untied his bindings. "Now, we were very lucky to find you washed up on the shore this mornin', so please—

I'm beggin' you—do as we tell you to." Banju stood, stretching his aching leg muscles. Bilk pushed him out of the tent. "Now get to work!"

He was led up a hill and finally saw what the other slaves were being forced to do; hundreds were building a tall wooden garrison while others were constructing what appeared to be the foundations of ten ships.

"It is very important that we build these as quickly as possible," Bilk said sternly. "The great and powerful Sarkk wants to invade Shallor within two months' time, so you get right to work and don't dare stop 'til we tell you." He pointed at a chest full of tools then began to walk back to the tent.

Banju quietly picked up a hammer and began to nail boards into one of the ships with the other slaves. *So Vince was right: Sarkk is planning to attack!* The temperature dropped within the next hour and dark gray clouds always concealed the sun. Banju briefly stopped to warm his hands and assess his surroundings for possible escape routes. The slavers' camp was surrounded by wide expanses of snowy plains and beyond that were mountains and volcanoes. There was no way for a man to quickly escape without being apprehended and most likely killed.

"If you're planning to escape," a slave said behind him, "forget about it. Jeth tried that last week and that's what happened to him." He gestured to a half-eaten corpse propped in the air by a spear. "We were forced to watch him get eaten by a Benkul's steed."

"A Benkul?"

"They're—"

Grud hit the slave with a club. "Back to work!" He hit him again, and the slave fell on his knees, blood dripping from his nose. Grud raised his club to hit him again when Banju intercepted it with his hammer. Before he could defend further, Grud kicked him in the stomach. "Stupid slave," he spat. "If we didn't need you so much, you would be dead where you lay."

Once Grud was out of sight, the beaten slave helped Banju to his feet. "Thanks; I don't think anyone has ever stood up for me like that before."

Banju winced. "Somebody must."

The slave forced a smile from his aching mouth as he resumed his work. "If more men were like you, we wouldn't be slaves anymore!"

The sun set with no further incident, and Banju was herded into a large pavilion with hundreds of other slaves. He and two other slaves shared a dirty fur blanket for warmth.

My hands...I can't feel my hands! Banju rubbed them together until life slowly crept back into them. He sighed and rested his head on a nearby post.

Now he could think. However, he soon realized that this was not necessarily good: Thoughts and images of Felicia flashed through his mind, filling him with a sense of emptiness and hopelessness the likes of which Banju had not felt since his father's death. He forced himself to think of something else before grief completely overcame his senses.

He still had the knife in his boot, but what could he possibly do with one knife? *Perhaps I could raise a coup.* The slaves far outnumbered their slavers, if only they would realize that! Now if only he could get his hands on a sword…

Crikkon. He missed its comforting presence on his back. What had become of it? Had Will taken it, or had the slavers done that themselves? *Don't worry, Father, I'll find it…if it's the last thing I'll do, I'll…*

He drifted into a fitful sleep.

"Rise and shine, you filthy animals!" Bilk announced. "The sun is nearly up, an' ye must reach King Sarkk's quota in three days' time!" He kicked the nearest groggy slave. "Come on, now, get up!"

The slaves all exited silently, ate a measly breakfast of dry bread and water and continued their monotonous work from the previous day. Banju worked until his arms could barely lift the hammer, but even then, he knew he could not rest for fear of getting beaten.

Unfortunately, an elderly man working near Banju did not have such endurance. He raised his hammer, and the momentum carried him backwards and to the ground. The man tried to lift himself up, but his arms gave out each time.

"Scum!" Grud exclaimed as he approached the struggling man. "Get up! Now!"

"I…I can't," the elder said in a winded and weak voice.

Grud snarled and kicked him. "Then you are worthless to us! If you refuse to get up," he lifted the man up by his hair and backhanded him in the face, "then stay down!" He began to strike him with a slender rod.

Banju could stand watching a helpless man being beaten no longer; he charged Grud and hit him as hard as he could in the back of the head with his hammer. He could feel Grud's flesh break open and his skull crunch as the hammer did not stop until it reached his brain tissue. He let go of the hammer, shocked by his first kill. The world around him blurred and his heartbeat quickened.

"Hey! Snap out of it!" a slave excitedly exclaimed beside him. "We need you!"

Banju returned to reality and realized that he had succeeded in starting a revolt. Slaves everywhere picked up whatever they could find—be it hammers, boards, nails or rocks—and began attacking their masters. Many slave managers fell in this assault; but even though they were greatly outnumbered, the slavers were better armed and trained. Archers began to pour out of wagons as Sarkk's men joined the fray. They shot any hostile slave and rounded every-one else to the center of the shipyard. The upheaval had ended just as quickly as it had begun.

Banju put his arms behind his head to admit defeat and was quickly bound before he could try anything else. Little did they know that he was secretly cutting his way out of his restraints with his hidden knife.

"You will all pay dearly for this petty rebellion," Bilk said angrily. "No food or water for the next two days and you will work nonstop until these ships and the barracks are finished. If you thought you were already livin' a terrible life, just wait unt—"

"The Undead Wanderer is approaching!" a sentry shouted in fear.

Bilk's furious and stern look turned into one of fear and dread. "Archers to the ready! Spear masters, charge him! Shielders, guard me!"

Banju watched as a lone man approached from the mountains. The spear masters mounted their horses and spurred them to run with all speed toward him. The first to reach him stabbed him with their spears, sending him roughly to the ground.

Well, that's the end of that man, Banju thought as he worked through his bindings.

Miraculously and shockingly, the man stood up, ripped the spears out of his chest and took out every one of the men with their own weapons.

Instead of doing their duty, the archers and the shielders turned and ran as fast as they could away from this incredible man. "Get back here, you cowards!" Bilk helplessly insisted. "Don't leave me here alone!"

One soldier obeyed his command and lifted a slave in hopes of using him as a hostage and human shield. Banju ripped out of his ropes and threw the knife so that the hilt hit the coward's temple.

He was about to charge at Bilk when the Undead Wanderer strode closer, and Banju unbelievingly recognized him as Will. Bilk grabbed a bow and shot arrow after arrow at him. Will barely reacted to the impacts and proceeded toward Bilk. "No, no, no! Don't kill me! Please! Go away! I-I didn't do anything wrong!" He hit Will with an axe, which embedded itself in Will's neck. Will gave him a chastising look, slowly removed the axe from his neck, and beheaded Bilk.

He sighed and rubbed his neck. "No, Bilk, you didn't do *any*thing wrong; you did *every*thing wrong." He turned to the stunned and frightened slaves. "You are all free. I would suggest that you get out of this cursed land as quickly as possible. Although, I can think of a certain heroic someone who needs more men to help him to defeat Sarkk." He winked at Banju. "Banju here is part of Shallor's Royal Army. Join him and you cannot only be free, but ensure the safety of Shallor and the free realms for years to come."

Some of the slaves left on horseback while many others stayed, interested by this proposition.

Will clasped and shook Banju's hand. "Glad to see you made it here alright!"

"You drugged and enslaved me!"

Will shrugged. "It got you here, didn't it?"

"I suppose…Say, how did you survive those deadly attacks?"

"Ah, that's my little secret."

"Will, after what you put me through, I think I deserve an explanation."

William sighed. "Alright, alright, you win, but only because I want to, not because you pressured me into it. And let me add that I would have told you that I was the Undead Wanderer earlier, but you cut off my list of names in our first meeting." Will tightened the strap around his sword. "Over three hundred years ago, before the fall of the Drifters and magicians alike during the Eradication, someone cursed me to live forever: never able to die from natural or unnatural causes. I was banished from Shallor—to return there would be worse than death—and was forced to sail across the sea. Since then, I have been exploring Makir, but unfortunately there isn't much to explore except for hot rocks and such."

"Why were you cursed?"

"I…I made someone *very* angry, and he had the means to make my life as miserable as he saw fit."

"So in short you're saying that he made you invincible?"

Will nodded sadly. "Yes, he did. I have tried many different times to end my sorrowful existence— like jumping into an active volcano—but nothing seems to work."

"I'm sorry, but isn't it sort of a gift as well as a curse?"

"I used to think so, mate, but when you see those you—" His voice broke for a moment. "—love dearly die while you live on unscathed without aging *is* a curse. I've seen many people die, Banju, some right in my arms."

Banju bowed his head. "I'm sorry, William. What I meant was that you could use this curse to help us defeat Sarkk and his army."

Will handed him a full canteen, two pieces of thick bread and a satchel. "Here, you should eat something. And your sword's in that satchel; thought it was too magnificent to risk the chances of it being confiscated by those filthy slavers, so I kept it."

He watched the remaining slaves prepare themselves for battle. "You know, you're right. I'll come with you, but mostly because I want to see old Sarkk finally get what he deserves. I have to warn you, though, I cannot kill Sarkk or any of his prized minions; I don't know why, but something stops me from being able to kill them, almost like they have a magical shield. No matter; I can still help bring down his army!" He unsheathed his sword and pointed it at the darkening sky, revealing a green blade. "Let the battle begin!"

Battle Lines

Banju, Will and the freed slaves took a shortcut by a river surrounded by tall dark mountains on both sides. The temperature began to slowly drop from cold to unbearably freezing.

Will had given Banju a special lightweight suit of armor that he claimed would keep Banju warm and comfortable in the intensifying cold. Banju was skeptical that it would work, but so far only his face felt the effect of the dropping temperature.

"Will, why is Makir covered in snow?" Banju asked. "In all of the stories I have heard, Makir is always described as being hot and barren."

"There is a highly scientifically logically reasonable explanation for that...I just haven't thought of it yet," Will said cheerfully as he continued to lead Banju and the slaves along the small path. "Ah yes! You see, when Sarkk rediscovered the Gauntlet, he used it to create an army. As he grew accustomed to its power, he began to use it to punish disobedient subjects: earthquakes, rainstorms, etc. Not to mention that he also tried to use it to make Makir a fertile land again. Well, the Gauntlet began to manipulate the landscape, and Nature didn't like that too much."

"So you're saying that the Gauntlet has created this negative effect on Makir?"

Will abruptly stopped their procession, deep in thought. He stood there for several seconds, making sure that he had explained it correctly. "Why, yes, that seems to be the gist of it." He pointed to the top of one of the dark hills. "That is where your Shallorian friends should be." Raising his voice, he said, "Everyone: please stay put while Banju and I go scout out the area. It is *essential* that all of you stay quiet; we don't know who or what might be nearby."

He motioned for Banju to follow him and together they stealthily made it to their destination. They didn't make it far before a deafening screech sliced through the air. "Lie flat on the ground now!" Will ordered.

Banju did as he said and placed a special shield Will had given him on his left arm and drew Crikkon. Will swiftly grabbed a strange looking bow from his back and removed his cloak. Many suspenseful minutes passed. "What was that?"

"It was a Benkul," Will explained, "three beast-flying magicians that Narkk convinced to follow him by giving them the ability to live forever. He did not make them invincible like me, mind you, but he made it so that they would never die from old age, sickness or other natural causes."

"So that dragon I saw before the Kry'vogh attacked…"

"That was *not* a dragon, but yes, it was one of them; most likely sent to stop your fleet from making it to Makir. Thanks to the Kry'vogh, there are only two Benkul left." He glanced around them and waved to the slaves. "Alright, I'd say that we're clear to go now. Just stay flat on the ground and follow me."

Banju was speechless when they reached the top; below them were the remains of a once huge wooden fort. Dead bodies were strewn around the ruins, not all of them enemies; the insignia of Shallor could clearly be seen in many places: an eagle with a dove flying beside it, both helping each other carry a sword. He followed the trail of blood and saw an army of armor up on a ridge miles away. "That's where we need to go. Come on!"

Will looked where he was pointing and pulled Banju back to their hiding place. "Not yet; there is something here."

"What do you mean?"

"I mean we're not alone." Will placed an arrow on his bow. "I'd put your helmet on if I were you."

Banju did as he suggested just as a giant bird passed over them. Banju realized it wasn't a bird at all, but one of the Benkul.

"Just stay down." Will aimed and waited for the beast to pass over them again then quickly released two arrows from his bow. The arrows hit the steed with such precision and intensity that it immediately began to fall from the sky.

"You did it!" Banju exclaimed.

Will shook his head. "No, I only killed the beast; it's the rider that I can't kill and he's the one that needs to be. Come on, we can go to your army now."

Banju followed him back to the top of the slope. "How fast can we get there?"

"How fast can you run?"

"Fast enough to run a marathon in a little over two hours."

"You're sure?" Will sounded surprised by this.

"Yes, I'm sure."

"Are you an elf?"

Banju chuckled. "No, I wish; I'm just human."

"Okay, I'll take your word for it. Unfortunately," he whistled to a horse that they had confiscated earlier, "we'll have to race each other another time; it is necessary for you to preserve your energy for the coming battle."

Banju reluctantly agreed and mounted the horse. "Where's yours?"

Will winked at him. "Don't you worry about me!" They then set off with Banju in front, Will running by his side and the slaves following close behind in their wagons. He was surprised when Will was soon ten yards in front of him. "Three centuries of practice, mate," Will remarked, gaining even more speed.

Banju spurred his horse to catch up, but could not come close to matching Will's high speed. He was nearly going too fast to stop when he saw Will halt; luckily, Banju recovered before he would have flown off the horse. They were just outside of the knights' camp.

"Who are you, and why are you here?" one of the sentries asked, wary of their small group.

Banju removed his helmet. "I am Sir Banju, the last surviving knight of the *Grandeur*. These people are my allies and have agreed to aid us in our battle."

The sentry eyed him suspiciously, then said, "Please, Sir Banju, come with me."

They followed the knight into one of the biggest tents—King Banton's tent, no doubt. Inside were many men that Banju recognized: Stonner, Captain Pikt, Lord Corbin, King Banton and others that Banju could only assume were military officers. He was surprised when he noticed that Vince was not present.

"Captain Banju," King Banton nodded his head in acknowledgment. All of the men were standing in a circle around a huge map of Makir. "It is a pleasure to see you alive and well. Might I ask what happened and why General Valerin is not with you?"

Banju bowed his head in deep respect and sorrow. "Sir, we were attacked by a sea monster on our way to Makir. All of us fought valiantly, but everyone died except for me." He gestured toward Will. "I would have died as well if not for this man."

"And who might you be?" King Banton asked in a curious tone.

Will stood proudly. "My name is William, but others call me—" One quick glance from Banju forced him to stop. "I am here to help you defeat Sarkk and his army."

"Mr. William, did you see this...sea monster attack the *Grandeur*?"

Will nodded. "Indeed I did, sire. My little raft wasn't fast enough to reach the *Grandeur* before it sank, so I decided to fish for survivors."

"I see." King Banton seemed unmoved by his story. "Tell me, William, do you have any military or combat experience?"

"Oh yes, sir, I have been practicing archery, swordsmanship and military tactics for the past—" Another glance from Banju stopped him once more. "—few years or so."

"Well then," King Banton said in a stern voice, "we would be happy to have another experienced gentleman among our ranks. We will provide you with a suit of armor—"

"Oh trust me, sir," Will interrupted, "that won't be necessary; I'll be just fine in the garments I'm wearing now."

King Banton had a surprised look on his face, though Banju could not tell if it was because he had been interrupted when he was speaking or because of Will's refusal. "And why is that?"

"Will has special abilities that make it so that he can't be harmed during battle," Banju explained, although by now their explanations probably sounded like an ill put-together tale.

King Banton turned his attention back to Will, eyebrow raised. "Care to elaborate?"

"Sure thing." Will grabbed a knife from one of the other tables and stabbed himself vigorously in the stomach. Many of the men in the tent gasped in surprise and shock. After stabbing himself dozens of times, Will held up the knife to reveal that there was no blood on it and put it back on the table. He bowed and raised his shirt to show that he did not have any cuts, gashes or scars. "You see, King Banton, I cannot be killed…by *anything*."

King Banton's mouth was agape, along with nearly everyone else's. "And…and you're willing to help us win this battle?"

"I am here to help, but I can't kill Sarkk or any of his prized minions; your soldiers will have to do that."

"Then we will accept your offer for help with open arms," King Banton said, a nervous smile coming to his lips.

"Thank you, King Banton," Will replied. Banju realized that no one had ever said King Banton's name and wondered how Will had known who he was. "Now may I ask what your plans are for this great siege?"

"Ah yes, Captain Pikt was just about to explain."

Captain Pikt stepped forward and pointed at a drawing of a castle on the map. "This is the castle where Sarkk is stationed. Our plan is rather simple: we go for a full frontal assault and take out the heart of Makir. We still have other legions of men coming from other sections of Makir to ensure that there are no hostile survivors. They will join us from the sides as soon as they can, thus catching the enemy in an enveloping maneuver." He paused for dramatic effect and to catch his breath. "Our main goal is to reach Sarkk and destroy the rumored Golden Gauntlet that he has allegedly found."

Will stepped up to the map. "A solid plan, Captain, but there are a few facts that you're missing that could be very useful in guaranteeing your victory. First off, if you do manage to destroy the Gauntlet, Makir will begin to sink into the sea. Don't ask me why, but I believe that most of it has to do with the fact that the Gauntlet has had an influence on this land for so long that if it's destroyed, most of Makir will be abolished as well. This way, you can send messengers to the other legions and tell them to come here immediately. Any and all other cities in Makir will be destroyed automatically if we do this right, which will make it so your men won't be directly responsible for the mass genocide of millions of people."

"Second, you're forgetting a strategic point that would have a better possibility of reaching Sarkk." He pointed behind the castle. "There is a narrow pass behind the castle called the Dragon's Mouth. It leads directly into a back entrance to Sarkk's castle. If you send a small squad of men into that pass, they might—just might—be able to take out Sarkk's reinforcements and possibly even sneak up behind Sarkk and kill him."

Catching on to his plan, Banju said, "With your leave, King Banton, I will lead the squad through the pass and into the castle. With any luck, we'll make it to Sarkk."

"Very well, Banju," King Banton replied after a moment of silent thought. "You have my permission to lead a group of men into the Dragon's Mouth. My son will assign men to your squad and you can leave when we begin our assault on the castle."

Banju bowed. "Thank you, King Banton."

With that, King Banton dismissed them so that the army could assemble. Stonner caught up to Banju and Will as they were heading for the supply tent. "Well, Banju, I hate to say 'I told you so,' but I told you so."

Will shook Stonner's hand. "It is a pleasure to meet you, Stonner, and it is good to see that someone else around here has a sense of humor."

"Uh…yeah, it's nice to meet you, too," Stonner replied with a confused smile. "How did you know my name?"

"It comes with the territory," Will explained.

The rest of their conversation was cut short when Vince came over and shook Banju's hand. "Glad to see you back in the ranks, soldier; we were beginning to think you were dead." Vince turned to face Will. "I know that your name is William, but who, exactly, are you?"

"He's a valuable asset to our army," Banju broke in.

"Excuse me," Will said impatiently, "I can speak, you know; I'm not a mute." He thrust his hand toward Vince. "You are correct: my name is Will. I'm what you people like to call... invulnerable."

Vince looked at Banju with a confused look on his face as he shook Will's hand. "Invulnerable? How, exactly?"

"Cursed," Banju stated.

"For three hundred years," Will added.

Vince released Will's hand and looked at his own nervously.

"Oh don't worry," Will said with a smile, "it's not contagious."

Vince heaved a huge sigh of relief. "Well, I am very glad that you decided to join us; I'm sure that you will be a pivotal ally in this battle."

"Just send me in first, that's all I ask. That way the enemy will waste all of their arrows and men on me."

"Sounds good to me." Vince looked up at the smoky sky. "I must be going now; I have a lot to get done before the battle."

"Very well," Will replied. "It was a pleasure meeting you, Prince Vince."

"And it was a pleasure meeting you as well, William."

They were left alone at the center of the large camp now, Banju preparing for his stealth assault and

Stonner getting ready for the front offensive. Will sat nearby, his shirt removed as he fished in his satchel for a clean one. Banju noted that he had several whiplashes on his back and dark red burns that spread from the back of his neck to his right shoulder blade. *All of his other previous wounds have healed instantaneously; perhaps he was whipped before he was cursed? A slave, maybe? I'll have to ask him when this is all over.* There was something that he wanted to ask him, though…

"William?"

"Yes?" Will had found his shirt and began to dress himself for battle.

Banju sat on a barrel across from Will. "How do you live with it?"

"Live with what?"

"With the death of your loved ones."

Will stopped what he was doing. "It is nigh impossible to fully live without them. Every time that I have lost someone, I feel as if I have also lost a part of myself. I then often isolate myself from the world, be it a mountain peak or the middle of the ocean. There comes a point, however, where I am able to let them go in a sense. Certainly the pain never leaves entirely, but I find that once I have recovered from their deaths, I am stronger in a way. It is as if they are with me…inside of me…and watching over me. Does that make sense?"

In a way, it did. Slightly comforted, Banju excused himself so that he could try to get some sleep.

He was nervous about this battle; it was going to be the first real battle he had ever been in, and he was afraid that he would not make it through alive. *Would death be so bad? I would be able to see my father and Felicia again. No, I can't think like that right now; I can't let my nerves get the better of me.* He drifted off into a restless sleep.

Someone blew a horn and a scout ran into King Banton's tent. Banju regretfully awoke and quietly stepped closer to the tent so that he could hear the report.

"Sir, Sarkk has gathered his forces in the valley in front of his fortress!" the scout was saying. "His numbers are increasing every other minute!"

"Inform all of the officers to arm their knights and stand at the ridge going into the valley," King Banton ordered.

"Yes, sir." The messenger rushed out of the tent and began to shout: "All hands to the ready! The battle begins now! The enemy is growing! All hands to the ready!"

Vince ran back to where Banju and his friends were standing. "Banju, your troops are ready for you. I would suggest taking them now before things erupt into chaos."

Banju saluted, put on his helmet and grabbed his shield. He glanced over at Stonner, who gave him a nod in farewell.

"Remember, Banju," Will said, "if you get close enough to Sarkk, destroy his Gauntlet and you will have brought victory to us all."

"I will," Banju promised. He then headed for the pass where a hundred knights were awaiting his instructions. The castle's tall dark spires made the fortress appear as if it were a crown that a titan had dropped from the sky.

"Sir," a knight on horseback gave him the reins to another steed. "Your horse."

"Thank you, Lieutenant." He mounted his horse and turned to face the men behind him. He could feel an air of despair and dread emanating from them. *It's time to give them a cause worth dying for,* he thought, remembering Valerin's words. "We are here today to bring down one of our long-time enemies. We have been given the task to take Sarkk's fortress. I know that many of you are uneasy; I'm nervous, too. For the majority of us, this will be our first battle. But remember one thing: We are not just doing this for ourselves; nay, we are doing this for our family, our friends, our future. The blood we spill today and whether we succeed in our assault will have an everlasting impact on the land we cherish. Let us fight as the knights of old! Let us fight for honor!" He heard a drum beat and trumpets blaring, indicating that the main force was going down into the valley. "They are depending on us to bring down the reinforcements. Now, let us go, let us fight" he drew

Crikkon and pointed it toward the fortress, "for peace and Shallor!"

At the Dragon's Mouth

The men cheered as they began their fast ride through the narrow pass. Banju sheathed Crikkon and took a lance that a knight to his right gave him. The entire front line had lances in case they met resistance outside of the castle. The castle was soon a foreboding dark wall in front of them, jagged rocks on either side jutting out as if it truly were a dragon's open jaw. He was about to shout something to raise the men's morale again when he saw a dark line of men waiting for them. "Lances at the ready!"

As they charged, so did their enemies. Adrenaline rushed through Banju as he braced for an enemy spearman. As the spearman stabbed out, Banju hit him hard with the lance and wrenched the spear out of his hands. He held the spear firmly and hit any enemy that came too close.

All was going well until a huge shockwave knocked nearly everyone off of their horses. Banju landed on a patch of sharp rocks with a thud.

"Banju," a voice whispered, "get up. Come on!" He was shocked to see his rival Velberk standing over him and offering him his hand. Banju took it and was about to stand when he heard Velberk gasp and saw an arrowhead protruding from his chest. "I...I don't understand!" He fell to the ground, never to rise again.

The attacker was thirty yards away and was quickly closing the gap.

Banju managed to stand and almost fell back down. The armor had protected him from most of the rocks, but a few had managed to stab him in the back. He grabbed his spear and faced this new enemy.

"You shall not go any farther!" the man said in a crispy voice. He wielded a dual-bladed weapon shaped like a staff and was wearing a dark blue cowl.

Banju thought about how he should proceed and the best way to fight this strange man. Out of all of the battle tactics that he knew, he chose to taunt his enemy first and evaluate any weaknesses he might have. "Hello, dark and mysterious man, how are you?"

The man growled. "Your friend killed my dragon."

"Oh, I see now: you're one of the Benkul. Well, if you want to exact your revenge on my friend, he's in the front."

"Don't take me for a fool," the Benkul spat. "I know who he is. Besides, those are not my orders. I can't kill your friend, but I can kill you!"

"You can try, my good man, but I'm afraid that you won't succeed."

The Benkul pulled back his cowl, revealing a skull devoid of flesh and skin with eerily glowing red eyes. "You should be afraid of me, boy!" He lunged forward.

Banju quickly drew Crikkon, blocked the powerful blow with it in his right hand, and stabbed at his assailant with the spear in his left. The Benkul managed to evade most of the spear but was not fast enough to stop it from cutting slightly through the right side of his chest. The Benkul howled and struck again.

This time the blow stunned Banju's right arm and made him drop Crikkon. He quickly blocked again with the spear, but the power behind the attack forced him to the ground. The spear was almost cut in half now, so he desperately searched the pass for the nearest weapon. All of the knights were still on the ground over a hundred yards away. What else could he use as a weapon? He rolled away from another strike, and that's when he saw it: the arrow stuck in Velberk's back less than five yards away.

He continued to roll away from the Benkul but was stabbed in the calf just inches away from his quarry. Banju screamed in pain and threw the blunt end of the spear at his assailant.

The Benkul deftly caught the projectile and hit Banju's chest with it. "You cannot win, boy."

"You underestimate the power of the young and resourceful." Banju yanked the arrow out of Velberk's corpse, buried it deep into the spot where the Benkul's heart should be and then roughly pulled it out and stabbed one of the Benkul's eyes. The Benkul fell to the ground and mysteriously turned into ash.

Banju sighed in relief and fell to the ground in exhaustion and pain. He thought for sure that he was going to die there until he heard many feet approaching.

"Sir, are you alright?" It was one of the last remaining knights. He cautiously opened his eyes and saw that it was Vren.

"I'm fine, Lieutenant, I just need a moment to regain my strength." Banju tore off a piece of his undershirt and tied it around his injured leg. "Status report?"

"All but a score of us dead, sir."

Banju stood to test his footing and was pleased to discover that he could still walk. Now if only the pain in his chest would go away. "We should continue our mission, then. The rest of the army is depending on us."

"We all agree with you, sir," Vren said, "and we will follow you until the end."

Banju smiled appreciatively. "Thanks, Vren; I have a feeling that you'll make a fine general someday."

"Thank you, sir."

"We'd better get going now," Banju said. "There is an entrance just a few hundred yards away."

The fortress loomed high above them, casting them in an almost pitch black shadow. They quietly made it into the castle and found that it was just as dark as it was outside. There were several passages to choose from and Banju had no idea which one to pick.

A headache, much like the ones he had experienced while fighting the araccia, suddenly struck him.

"Are you alright, sir?" Vren asked.

"Yes, it's only a headache." He could not explain it, but somehow he knew that they had to go down the corridor to the left. "Let's try the left one; it may lead us to the front gate." The men obeyed without hesitation. He felt guilty about not telling them about the wizard that they would soon meet, but he figured that it might raise suspicion. Hopefully this newfound intuition was not leading them all into a trap.

Just as he had predicted, a wizard soon approached from one of the other corridors and stopped them. "Who are you and what are you doing here?" he asked.

Banju thought it best to tell him the truth. "We have come to take this fortress and bring peace and prosperity to Shallor."

"You are foolish to enter with such few men!" The wizard muttered something and Banju and all of his men froze in place. "You are all as good as dead now!" The wizard began to laugh evilly but was cut short when a sword struck him from behind. When he fell, Banju could see that their rescuer was wearing a dark green cloak and had short dirty-blonde hair and green eyes.

"I apologize that you had to be stopped like that," their rescuer said as they unfroze. He offered Banju his hand. "The name's Luke."

Banju shook it. "Banju. May I ask what you are doing here?"

"I am a sorcerer here, Sir Banju. That wizard on the floor was my mentor, one of the best of the best. I have grown tired of the cruelty of Makir and wish to accompany you on the rest of your mission and return with you to Shallor. With your permission, of course."

Banju thought deeply about this. If Luke was telling the truth, he could be a valuable ally to their squad and to the preservation of Shallor. That is, if people with the Eradication still fresh in their minds would accept a magic user. But if he was lying... "You can help us if you wish, Luke. Could you please tell me where a strategic position in the front of the castle would be?"

Luke grinned and waved his hand toward the corridor that he had emerged from. "Follow me."

"Sir Stonner, watch out!"

Stonner moved out of the way just in time to avoid a throwing axe. He raised his bow and shot the goblin that had thrown it. A man charged Stonner and struck down with his scimitar, and Stonner quickly intercepted it and stabbed the man. Stonner winced as he heard his sword come into contact with flesh and bone.

The battle was not going well for the army of Shallor; it seemed that Sarkk was creating two or three creatures for every one killed. Much of the army had already fallen and the man closest to Sarkk was Will. It was a pity that he could not kill their enemy, but thankfully he could kill many of the beasts that Sarkk was producing with the fabled Golden Gauntlet. Stonner hoped that Banju and his squad would successfully take the fortress; otherwise the battle would be over *very* quickly.

He put two arrows on his bow and shot them directly at a huge troll's face. Knights yelled with excitement as the giant fell and they charged forward only to be killed by a torrent of black arrows.

Stonner growled in impatience and saw that the culprit firing the arrows was flying high above the battle on a dragon. Stonner aimed and pulled the bowstring as far back as it would go. The arrow shot off with a satisfying *twang* and hit the Benkul square in the chest. There was a shriek, and then the dragon began to spiral down toward a patch of huge, sharp rocks. Stonner did not remember hitting the dragon, but then he realized that dozens of other archers had taken his lead and shot the beast at the same time that he had hit the Benkul. When the dragon pierced the rocks there was a huge shockwave that sent Stonner and many others to the ground.

Perhaps this battle is looking up for us, he thought with a smile as he threw a knife at an approaching goblin.

"There is a balcony outside of this door," Luke said. "It should be right above the battle and close to Sarkk."

"Thank you, Luke," Banju replied. They had met little resistance in the castle; and when they had, Luke had pretended to still be on the guards' side and kill them. In Banju's opinion, that had been the only thing that had gone right that day. He turned to his men. "How many of you are good with a bow?"

"Ten of us, sir," Lieutenant Vren stated.

"Alright, when we get on the balcony I want five archers on either side of me ready to fire on my signal. The rest of you will follow Luke to the entrance to the castle. I want you out of the entrance as our cover, but don't run out until you see the archer's arrows. Understood?"

The men saluted in unison. "Yes, sir!"

"Then let's take down Sarkk and finally bring peace to Shallor!"

He beheaded a man, pierced a troll's throat and fired arrows at a fleeing group of men on horseback, all while not noticing that a spearman had sneaked up behind him and stabbed him in the back. He spun around and in one fluid motion hit the spearman under his chin with his bow. An arrow lodged itself in his right shoulder and he returned the favor by hitting the archer with the same arrow that had been fired.

No one was going to stop Will, for he could not be stopped—only slowed down for a time. Unfortunately, Sarkk's men had yet to realize that simple truth.

A lucky arrow managed to hit him in the head, slightly making him flinch. He pulled it out and threw it at a man who was attempting to kill a knight. The knight thanked him and resumed battle with a new foe.

Will cursed as a giant tree root smashed out of the ground and violently pushed him hundreds of feet away. Knights screamed in pain and terror as tree roots came out of the ground and crushed, hit or tore them apart. In a land nearly devoid of trees, Will suspected that this had to be the handiwork of Sarkk and his Golden Gauntlet. *Curse those elves and dwarves who made it!*

He picked up a large axe from a fallen troll and charged the growing tree roots, hacking away at anything that did not look human. The last root was just getting axed when he heard the sound of thousands of pounding horses' hooves over the roar of the battle. Will quickly glanced at both sides of the battlefield and breathed a sigh of relief. Shallor's reinforcements had arrived.

"Charge forward, men! For Shallor!" Vince shouted to his troops when it seemed that they needed more morale. From where he was fighting, he knew why: knights were falling left and right and it appeared as if the enemy line was never breached. If progress was not made soon, he was afraid that *he* would be the one that would need more confidence.

Come on, Banju, where are you? It had been nearly a full day since Banju had been sent out and this battle had begun. Now he doubted their judgment on sending Banju on that mission with just a hundred men to complete a task that should take thousands more.

He parried a blow and struck his opponent across the head. Dread rushed through him as a wall of flame incinerated the knights in his line of vision. When the cloud of smoke vanished, he saw a man wearing a dark red cloak and cowl and holding a bloodstained dual-bladed weapon shaped like a staff in his left hand.

A knight charged him but was blown back by a strong gust of hot air. The powerful man—or whatever it was—walked slowly forward, killing any knight that got in his way.

Vince knew who he was heading for—his father was fifty yards behind him fighting with a different squad. *You won't reach my father alive, you beast!*

As if reading his thoughts, the man shifted his gaze upon him and shot a huge fireball at Vince; it passed close enough by him that he could feel the heat emanating from it.

Time seemed to slow as he helplessly watched the ball of flame hit his father in the chest. He shouted and tears filled his eyes; King Banton the Third was dead.

Anger welled within Vince and he yelled and shot an arrow at his father's killer. The being must have been caught of guard—or he wanted it to happen—for the arrow pierced his concealed face. It shouted in pain and surprise and then tumbled over. Vince dismounted his horse, went over to the man and stabbed him several times to make sure that he was dead. He would have continued stabbing the killer if Captain Pikt had not put a comforting yet stern hand on his shoulder.

"He's dead, Vince," Captain Pikt said, although Vince was unsure whether he meant that his father or the killer was dead. "Shallor needs you now; it needs you to be its king and fight valiantly today to bring peace to us all."

Vince sighed, releasing some of his tension. "You're right, Captain, Shallor *does* need help." He looked up at the dark fortress. "But I fear that none of us will be returning to Shallor if Banju doesn't take that castle."

Banju gingerly stepped onto the balcony and stood amazed at the battle taking place beneath him. From his viewpoint it looked as if Sarkk's forces were overpowering King Banton's. *If I don't act soon, there won't be any hope of victory.* He grimaced as he watched tree roots tear knights in half and the ground open up and swallow a score more.

He slowly stepped closer to the edge of the balcony and peered below him. Sarkk was laughing with pleasure as he continually spawned creature after creature out onto the battlefield. Sarkk's right hand was raised and was glowing in a glorious gold color, the essence of the Golden Gauntlet.

What could Banju do from such a height? He could jump, but that would surely kill him. *I'm prepared to die for peace, Banju. Are you?* Valerin's last words to him rang in his ears. *I suppose we're about to find out, General.*

"Archers, are you in position?" Banju quietly asked behind him.

"We're in position, sir," one of the archers confirmed. "Bows loaded and ready to fire at the target on your command."

"Perfect." Banju exhaled and tried to calm his breathing for what he was about to do. He unsheathed Crikkon, gripped it tightly and then tightened his grip on his triangular shield. *Now if only my helmet hadn't fallen off during the Benkul encounter. Ah yes, I forgot, I need to have Crikkon sheathed.* The sword returned to its sheath on his back. "Here we go, men."

Banju stood on the railing of the balcony and held his shield with both hands. *This is it…*

What in the name of Shallor is he doing? Stonner thought while he struck a deathly blow to his former opponent. *Why would Banju stand on the top of a balcony where all the archers in the area can see him?*

Aside from Will, Stonner and his squad were the only men close to the fortress. However, he barely had time to wonder what Banju was doing, for Sarkk looked directly at him and smiled. Stonner smiled back, but soon realized that something else was not right: the creatures within a three hundred meter radius of Sarkk ran as far away as they could, leaving Stonner a clear path to Sarkk. *Oh, great! A trap!*

The glowing Golden Gauntlet on Sarkk's right hand pointed at Stonner, and he heard a hissing sound come from behind. Stonner turned and saw three giant snakes ten feet away, their tongues slithering in his direction.

"Hello there." Stonner shot an arrow into the open mouth of the center snake, but never had the chance to try again, for the other two snakes lurched forward, just barely missing Stonner's face. He drew his sword and cut off the tongue of one of the snakes and then ran for the cover of a group of boulders. The tongue-less snake writhed in pain and knocked into the other one.

Stonner searched his environment for anything he could use besides his sword. He picked up a large rock and hurled it at the snake that still had its tongue. The snake briefly recoiled as the rock hit it on the head. He laughed victoriously, but it was cut short when the tongue-less snake slithered into the boulders. Without its tongue, it was half blind, but

Stonner was not going to take any chances. He grabbed a spear and pushed deep under the tongue-less snake's chin, killing it instantly...or so he thought. Its death throes battered most of the boulders to bits, nearly crushing Stonner in the process.

When it finally stopped moving, he cautiously stood up and looked for the last snake. He almost swore when he noticed that he was right next to the lava river coming out of a nearby volcano. *That snake must have hit me harder than I thought!*

There was a hiss, and the last snake appeared behind its dead companion and extended its body to its full height, towering above Stonner.

"The first thing you learn in battle," Stonner said, more to himself than to the snake, "is to never show off while in a duel with an unfamiliar opponent; it makes you too vulnerable." He revealed the axe that he had been hiding in his left hand and hit the snake's neck as hard as he could. The serpent hissed in pain and tried to snap at him before its head fell from the rest of its body. "Clearly, you never learned that lesson."

Banju braced himself and jumped, shield raised, off of the balcony. Sarkk, with his back to the castle, had no warning before the shield hit him in the back of the head. It felt like hitting a granite wall, nearly breaking Banju's arms in the attack. He fell off of Sarkk's back, but Sarkk remained standing.

He turned around and faced his assailant. "A brave yet foolish attempt." Sarkk kicked Banju in the stomach, sending him flying. "Now you will know what true pain feels like."

Banju stood up, holding his left hand to his stomach. "You…cannot…win!" He coughed up blood.

Sarkk chuckled and clenched his fists. "My boy, don't you know that you have already lost?" He punched Banju in the jaw, pushing him to the ground. "Please, before I kill you, tell me your name."

Banju breathed heavily and could feel the blood gushing out of his mouth. He gathered his strength and stood up defiantly, staring Sarkk right in his glowing orange eyes. "M-my name …my name is…is…Banju."

The confident smile left Sarkk's face and was replaced by a slight hint of fear. "Banju, eh? I know your kind." He picked up Banju so that they could see levelly eye to eye. "That will make killing you even more enjoyable." He threw Banju roughly up against the fortress wall. "For a man of your heritage I would have expected something a little more…challenging."

Banju could feel his strength and life slowly ebbing away. He tried to push himself back up, but failed. "S-sorry to… disappoint."

Sarkk stomped over to him, stabbed a small spike into his side and threw him away from the fortress. Banju feared that he was going to die before the rest of the plan could come into action. He felt

279

hopeless, ready to give in to the darkness threatening to overcome him.

As death drew nearer, his mind wandered away from the battle. The sounds of metal against metal and the screaming of men slowly ebbed away until he was enveloped in blissful silence. He saw Felicia as he desperately tried to prevent her from being pulled into the water by the Kry'vogh. Tranquility and longing filled his heart and mind. *"Everything is going to be okay, Banju. You can do this."*

"I can't," he cried. *"Not without you."*

She smiled at him, that smile that always made his heart skip a beat. *"Yes you can. You need only let me go."*

"No, I'll never let you go! I won't lose you again."

"You must, Banju. Only after you let go will you be able to live."

"Life is not worth living without you."

She tapped his hand. *"I will always be a part of you, but you must realize that we were never meant to grow old together. We will have a chance to see each other again, but not in this life. But now, you need to let me go."*

Tears fell from his face and down to the water below. *"I love you."*

"And I love you." Her voice dropped to a whisper. *"It is time for me to leave. Will you let me?"*

Conflictions erupted in his mind, but he managed to say, *"Yes."*

"Good. Until we meet again, my lover."

He then let her go, the smile returning to her lips; and as she hit the water, his surroundings shattered, taking with it the despair and depression that he had acquired after Felicia's death. Immensely relieved, he now found himself back at home cradling his father right before his death.

"Father," he said with joy.

"It seems that death has taken me from you, Banju. I never had a chance to tell you how proud I am to be your father. And now you're a knight, like you always wanted to be. Well done!"

"You don't know how much it means to hear you say those words."

Thanju winked. "I have a pretty good idea. Now come: you have a battle to finish."

"But I can't defeat him, father; he's too powerful."

"Nonsense! You are my son. You can accomplish anything you put your mind to; just look at how far you've come since leaving the village! You can defeat this man." His father began to fade, and as he did, he repeated the words he had told Banju on the dark shore. "Stay strong, son, and whatever you do, don't give up." Banju returned to the battle, free of the doubt and desperation that he had had only moments before. Energy and strength surged back into him and he was able to stand and remove the spike. "Never give up," he said out loud.

"Surprising," Sarkk muttered as he began to menacingly approach Banju again, his gauntlet hand slightly twitching. "A normal human being would have given up minutes ago. But you are not normal, are you?"

Banju looked over Sarkk's head onto the balcony. *I just need to give the signal.* "It will take more than a few throws to stop a man with a high resolve." He drew Crikkon and pointed the blade at the balcony. The sword seemed to shimmer with a golden-blue light. "For Shallor!"

Ten arrows lodged themselves in Sarkk's back, but he only winced for a heartbeat and continued heading for Banju. He chuckled. "Your petty arrows are no match for my might!" He pointed the Golden Gauntlet at the balcony and a flock of crows appeared out of thin air and attacked the archers. "I wish that you would have thought about that, Banju."

He reached for Banju, but stopped when a giant snakehead hit him in the face.

"Leave him alone!" Stonner called from close by, shooting arrows into Sarkk's chest.

Taking the opportunity, Banju brought Crikkon down on Sarkk's left arm. The blade barely made it through his armor, but it did manage to cut off a strange black plant that Sarkk had had wrapped around his arm.

At first the evil king stood in shock, a single tear falling down his disfigured face. "You killed her!" Sarkk growled in anger, raised the Gauntlet and hit the ground, creating a shockwave that sent Stonner and Banju flying.

Banju grunted as he landed on top of a pile of small boulders right next to a flowing lava river. An idea sprang to his mind. He picked up a rock and threw it at Sarkk.

Sarkk caught the rock, cast it aside and continued walking toward Banju.

"Come on...just a little closer," Banju murmured to himself and threw another barrage of rocks. Sarkk blocked most of them, but one was lucky enough to hit him on the nose. He yelled and picked up his pace.

Banju got up and ran down closer to the lava, hoping that his attacker would follow. Sarkk stopped very briefly in thought and then followed Banju down to the bank of the lava river. Banju sprinted as fast as he could—which was not as fast as he would have liked, given his injuries—and ran back up a portion of the bank. A stream of hot water erupted out of a geyser thirty yards behind him.

"It's over, Sarkk!" He shouted over the roar of the river and the erupting geyser. "Surrender now!"

Sarkk snarled and placed himself in a position a few feet lower on the bank. "Yes, it is over! Unfortunately, I will not be the one dying or surrendering today—" the Gauntlet glowed in Banju's direction. "—you will!"

Acting so fast that he barely had time to think, Banju slashed Crikkon through Sarkk's right arm. Black blood gushed out of his limb, and Sarkk screamed; the Golden Gauntlet fell to the steaming ground and stopped glowing.

Banju flipped off of the rock that he had been standing on and kicked Sarkk solidly in the chest with both feet, sending the latter into the lava flow. Sarkk screamed one last time before he disintegrated into his final resting place.

Banju fell to his knees and let out the breath that he was not even aware that he had been holding. The battle was over, and he had succeeded in defeating the undefeatable. He felt a reassuring presence behind him.

"You did it, Banju," Stonner said. "You killed him, acquired the Gauntlet *and* possibly brought peace to Shallor. Not to mention the fact that you successfully managed to do a flip! Come on; grab the Gauntlet and we'll go join up with the others."

Banju shook his head. "We cannot keep the Gauntlet, Stonner; it has been a symbol of evil for too long. Its power would only corrupt whoever wore it." Visions of a desolate Shallor flashed through his mind. Banju threw the Golden Gauntlet into the river and stood up, regretting it as he did so; his gut felt like it had a dozen swords stuck in it. "We need to inform King Banton that it is time to leave." Will's warning of Makir's destruction began to nag at him.

Lieutenant Vren and Luke greeted them when they returned to the battlefield.

"Area secure, sir," Lieutenant Vren said in confidence.

"Thank you, Lieutenant." Banju glanced at where the battle should have been taking place but was shocked to see hundreds of thousands of dead bodies strewn in all directions.

"When Sarkk died, all of his creations died, as well," Luke explained. "And what men were not his handiwork lost confidence and were quickly slain. The rest of Shallor's army is heading for the harbor, just as Will suggested."

"Then we must join them," Banju stated as he limped in the direction that he had originally came with Will.

"Aye, but not that way." Banju spun around and eyed Lieutenant Vren suspiciously. "The king left horses for us to return on," Vren continued with a smile.

They mounted the horses and rode off to find the fleet. *The battle is over,* Banju thought as relief showered over him.

ooo

A Battle Lost, a War Won

The halls were dark, hot and musty. No one enjoyed going down them, which could be a prime reason the halls had been left the way that they were. He walked down them anyway, hoping to please his master with his courage. That was a long stretch, he knew, but it was worth a try. After all, the news that he was about to give was going to make his master *very* furious. If it came to that, he hoped that he would not be in the chamber when the rampage came; for when it came, people would die.

He swore as he tripped and almost fell on his injured leg. It had been a couple months since the arrow had gotten him in his left calf, but it still hurt as if it had happened just days before. *Death to that boy and his allies!* His right iron index finger twitched uncontrollably in fury until he stopped it with his free hand. Having a metal finger was not that bad, but it constantly reminded him of that fateful night when his crew had decided to rob two "harmless" boys.

Never again will I underestimate you, he said to the boy as if he could hear him, *Next time we meet, you'll be the one with lost limbs.* He chuckled as he remembered the look on the boy's face when he had slit the girl's throat. *At least I had the satisfaction of causing you some pain.*

He picked up his pace as he heard the distant cathedral bells ringing. Time for his meeting, and he was going to be late. Perhaps his master was not going to be impressed by his courage after all.

The huge doors creaked eerily as he opened them. He entered the viewing chamber and was impressed by the ingenuity of its design. It was circular, five hundred feet in diameter and the ceiling was three hundred feet above him. Every two meters the wall cut out into a clear rectangular window nearly half the height of the chamber, giving the room the illusion that it was even bigger than it really was.

At the very center of the chamber, the stone floor declined into a bowl shape ten feet in diameter and three feet deep, which many called the meditation circle. There, sitting cross-legged in the middle, was his master.

Stories about men being killed for interrupting the master's meditation filled his mind. He gulped and mustered all of his courage into breaking his master's trance. "M-master? I bring news from your scouts."

His master did not move, his back still toward the bandit leader. "Which scouts? Speak up, Jareb, so that I can hear you."

That voice, Jareb thought, *just like they said: smooth and calm.* He knew that his master was just testing him; after all, how could a man with such great power be dumb and deaf? "The scouts you sent to observe Makir, my lord."

His master rose and turned to face him, revealing the gruesome scar on the left side of his face. A slight smile crossed his lord's lips. "And?"

Jareb began to brace himself for the expected result of the coming news. "S-Sarkk has been defeated, sir. Makir has been reported to be falling into the sea!"

There was a moment of miserable silence, and Jareb hoped that his master would soon break that spell. He did, but not in the way that Jareb had expected: he laughed.

"Excellent!" his master said with a wide smile. "This is what I had hoped for, but I did not expect that the boy would be able to pull it off so beautifully!"

"I...I don't understand, sir."

"With Makir gone, Shallor will think that they have finally brought peace to their pathetic land." His smile grew wider, causing parts of the scar to look as if they were going to break off of his face. "But they have been deceived for centuries now." His master moved to one of the windows and gazed at the thunderstorm raging on outside. "No more will we be stuck in this despicable land of eternal rain. No more will my people starve. No more will Shallor stand! Makir has lost a battle today, but we have won a great victory!"

Jareb was shocked by this unforeseen outcome. "You...you are not mad at me, sir?"

His master's cool eyes bore into him. "I am not mad at you for delivering such good news." He stepped closer to Jareb until their faces were nearly a foot apart. "I am, however, furious that you failed to conquer the small village in the valleys and for utterly failing to capture the boy. But do not fret, Jareb; the Dragon Lord shall rise and destroy him, just as he defeated the Drifters."

A sharp, hot pain rose in Jareb's stomach and spread to his chest and arms. "It is a pity," his master continued, "that you will not be able to see it happen."

The last thing that Jareb saw before falling into oblivion was his master staring calmly at him with his cold blue eyes.

ooo

Moving On

Waves rocked the *Majestic* as Makir's mountains slowly began to collapse into the ocean. The dark clouds surrounding Makir began to clear, revealing a beautiful blue sky and glorious sunshine. Despite the warmth, Banju shivered. He had almost single-handedly destroyed an entire civilization.

A candle-shield passed by beneath him; since not all of the bodies of the fallen could be acquired before Makir's destruction, the Shallorian troops had placed shields in the water and lit candles atop them to commemorate their departed comrades. Luke had used magic to ensure that the shields would stay afloat and the candles lit and had produced white flower pedals to follow the candle-shields. Thousands of candles had been lit.

Banju heard a sword being drawn and turned to see Vince placing it in his father's hands on King Banton's makeshift open casket. The former king lay on a bed hung up by nets on the *Majestic's* forward deck, his crown and armor glistening a bright gold and his face serene as if he were in a deep sleep. Joining in on the ceremony, the other ships surrounded the *Majestic*. Each ship's deck was filled with morose and weary men. The battle had been won, but at the cost of their king's life and thousands more.

Vince said not a word, standing before his father and staring without really seeing. The silence was so complete that Banju could hear the sails flapping in the wind and the waves lazily hitting the sides of the ships. This lasted for several minutes before Vince snapped out of his trance and addressed the battle-worn crew, his voice strong enough to be heard on the other ships:

"We lost a great many men today. The battle was fierce, the enemy immense." Vince turned away from his father and faced his men, his eyes red and his jaw set. "And yet, against all impossibility, we came out victorious. Let us never forget this day, and the friends and family who sacrificed their lives for Shallor." At this his gaze flickered back to his father. "We lost the greatest of men, but I pray that we will not lose the greatness that they upheld.

"As you all know, the law dictates that upon a king's death that his son will inherit the throne, but it also states that the people may choose another if they deem the king's son unworthy. I lay myself before you today in the wake of our enemy's destruction to decide for the betterment of our kingdom." Finished, Vince's knees seemed to collapse from underneath him and he knelt before his father.

The fleet was quiet once more. Banju considered this prospect; prior to Vince's family, the last change of royal bloodlines had led to King Leron's quick demise—to do so now would likely have the same result. And yet no one stepped forward. *I suppose that there is only one thing left to do.*

Banju drew Crikkon, bowed his head and knelt before Vince. At first nothing happened, but then Stonner and Vren did the same, then Luke and Will and then the air was filled with the sound of swords being drawn. Banju looked to his left and right and saw that every man was kneeling and that Vince's sorrowful expression was now mixed with gratitude and joy.

"Rise," the king said.

With the decision made, everyone resumed watching the candle-shields float toward the sunken Makir.

Beside Banju, Stonner said, "I can't believe we did it, and we survived, no less."

"Surviving is only half the battle," Will commented.

"Indeed," Stonner replied.

Banju picked up a spare shield, placed a candle upon its inside and walked over to Luke. "Could you make this like the others?" he asked.

Nodding, Luke took the shield, mumbled a few indistinguishable words and waved his hand over the candle. It suddenly burst into a majestic blue flame. "Would you like me to send it into the water, as well?"

"No, I will do that myself." Banju moved to the lowest point on the deck. *For Felicia, for my father, for Terin, for Velberk, for the crew of the* Grandeur, *for the girl in the village.* He dropped the shield into the water; after it landed with a small splash, it evened out and headed for the other memorials. *May the afterlife bring you all peace.*

His blue flame joined with the red, green and gold flames of the others as the rest of Makir crumbled into the sea. So many lives had been extinguished, and for what? The possibility of peace and security? Banju wondered if peace would truly come. *It came to me,* he thought. *It can surely return to Shallor; it may just need a little help along the way.*

And then, like a hammer striking an anvil, realization hit him: After centuries of conflict, Shallor was going to be a free and peaceful land once more. A ray of hope flashed through Banju as he prayed that it would remain peaceful for a long, long time.

ACKNOWLEDGMENTS

Much like many other adventures, this one would not have been possible without the unwavering support of my friends and family.

I would like to thank my parents for always being there (though I kept much of this manuscript a secret from them), as well as my older sister who provided me with the stunning "frozen wasteland" pictures of Lake Michigan used in the first edition of the book. A special thank you to my Uncle Ken for providing me with the beautiful ocean shot used for the cover of the paperback. I am also thankful for my Aunt Nichole who showed an interest in my very first draft when I was eleven and *Battle Lines* was called *Banju: Son of Hercules.* It was her interest in my book that inspired me to turn a fifteen-page notebook story into a full-fledged novel.

Now let's get to the good stuff: a huge thank you to those who helped me through the long and ever-changing road of book writing. To my best friend Ben Prout, for reading my rough draft of *Battle Lines* (known simply as *Banju* back then) and giving me suggestions on how to improve and also for having an open mind whenever I ran an idea by him. Without him the final battle would have only been a three-page ordeal told from Banju's perspective and the last chapter would have been a plethora of clichés. To my incredible 9th Grade English teacher Mrs. Suzanne Seacord who read and fixed portions of my second draft and told me that the story "needed some romance." To my friend Skyler Benn who helped me realize that one does not simply land a raft onto Makir. To Jessica Mills for reading bits and pieces of my final draft (including the unplanned expansion of Rik's story) and always encouraging me with her enthusiasm and honesty. To my amazing 10th, 11th and 12th Grade English and eventual Creative Writing teacher Mr. Chad Broughman for critiquing my first few chapters and helping me realize that adding a scene where Elaine actually fights her killer to the death might be a good dramatic twist; and thank you for improving my writing style over the years and opening my eyes to a whole new world in Creative Writing class; I realize that much of this text likely has grammatical errors and is not "Broughmanesque," but it would have been a lot worse had I not been consistently pushed to improve my writing style in his classes. Thank you to all others who have encouraged me and I have not mentioned—to do so would be a novel in and of itself; many may not realize it, but everyone I come in contact with impacts my stories in some fashion or another.

A special thank you to Dakota S. for helping me develop the honorable Stonner all those years ago and to my good friend Kasen Hollingsworth for being the living embodiment of this character.

No story would have been possible without the support, inspiration and people that the true Creator of All provided me.

Additionally, I am grateful for other authors who inspired me to create my own world. First and foremost, thank you to the late J.R.R. Tolkien for writing *The Lord of the Rings* and admittedly inspiring the majority of my very first draft. To Christopher Paolini and his *Inheritance Cycle* for showing me when I was still a teen that it is indeed possible to write and publish a book at a young age. To George R.R. Martin for creating the enthralling *A Song of Ice and Fire* series and helping me realize that not all "good" characters need to have a happy ending.

And last but not least, thank you to you, the reader. I hope you enjoyed this story and will return with me when *Battle Lines'* sequel *Battlefront* is published in two or three years' time. I promise to deliver an even deeper, more magical tale in Banju and Shallor's continuing quest for tranquility.

A storm is brewing on the dark horizon, but serenity is only a cloud break away.

Many thanks and may peace find you and yours,

Andrew Furstenberg

Questions? Comments? Critiques? Feel free to contact me at:

Email: quest4tranquility@hotmail.com

or

On Facebook @ facebook.com/peace4shallor

Made in the USA
Lexington, KY
10 January 2014